*Tempe...*

Kate Valent

VALIANT INK

To Dad. I wish life had given us more time to drink tea together.

Contents

Prologue

Dear Miss Graham,

I'm sorry to inform you that your book INTO THE OVEN is not a good fit for Chapman and Hall's list at this time. I'm afraid we found the story unable to stand beside *The String of Pearls.*

Sincerely,
Edward Chapman and William Hall

Dear Miss Graham,

We are passing on INTO THE OVEN. While it would be a riveting serial, it is too similar to another work on our list, *The String of Pearls.*

Sincerely,
Edward Lloyd

Miss Graham,

We're passing on this one.

Alfred Harmsworth

Chapter 1

The barber pulled out a straight razor, the blade sharp enough to slit a man's throat. Charlotte paused as she set a tray of rolls down on the counter of her family's bakery. The white shaving cream smeared across the man's chin made it impossible to tell his age, but he looked at ease in the chair as if he never suspected his barber could kill him on a whim. Without pausing the barber lifted the razor to the man's throat and slid it across his neck with deft swiftness, blood spraying—

No, no, he couldn't very well do that. Not when anyone walking past could see through the shop's window and witness him killing a man. Not to mention Charlotte watching from across the street. It would take her all of five minutes to dash out the back door of the bakery and report the murder to the bobbies.

All the more reason to respect Mr. Todd's foresight in having a trap door to the basement in the penny blood serial The String of Pearls. Breaking a man's neck by sending him crashing into the basement wasn't as dramatic as always using a razor, but it kept the dirty business out of sight. Unlike Mr. Todd, Mr. Housen would never kill one of his customers. It was bad for business.

"Thank you for the rolls," Charlotte's mother said, breaking her out of her reverie. "Mrs. White should be here any minute to pick these up. How is our last order coming along?" She scratched off Mrs. White's name on her order list. Her mother wore her hair tied back in a neat bun. Not a speck of flour spotted her apron. She preferred to spend her time at the front of the shop instead of in the kitchen. The kitchen was the domain of Charlotte's father.

"Everything should be ready in time." Everything had been running well all day. Too well. It made Charlotte feel like she was forgetting something important. Her father's head assistant baker had quit last month, lured in by a generous offer to work in a duke's kitchen. Each day since had been a struggle to get back to running smoothly.

"Perfect. Your father should have the fresh order of flour here within the hour. He'll need you to keep your cousin away from the bags. Lord knows what a mess Clod could make with it all."

Charlotte froze. So that was what she'd forgotten, her cousin Claude. With the head assistant gone, her parents had agreed to give him a chance to fill the gap. The poor lad had been cursed at a young age when his father got into dabbling with magic he didn't understand to climb the social ladder. The family had called him Clumsy Clod since. His father's magic career ended with nothing but a cursed son to show for his efforts.

Claude was far from the last man in the city rumored to be cursed from unskilled magic. But with poverty rampant, plenty of people fell into the temptation of trying untested or dangerous magic in the hopes of escaping the factories or workhouses. Until recently there'd been no books available to the commoners to teach them safe magic. Only rumors, unfinished books, and fake spells floating about. No one in the family knew how her grandfather had managed to get a hold of the spell they used in the bakery.

The bell over the door dinged, alerting them to a new customer. A man in a smart suit strolled inside. One of the local solicitors with a habit of wearing his cravat crooked.

"Quick, get into the back." Her mother shoved her through the door before she could protest. Charlotte took it as an aggressive reminder to not let gentlemen see her covered in flour. She didn't mind, though. It gave her time to catch up on her reading instead of letting her mother parade her around to parties.

She closed her eyes and took a deep breath before opening them. Claude yelped and several eggs went flying upward until they crashed into the ceiling. They'd never figured out what his curse was, but whatever it was it made the boy clumsier than anyone Charlotte had ever met. At seventeen he'd tripped and dropped enough eggs for two lifetimes already. But somehow his clumsiness always worked out in the end. For baking at least. He was still learning, but every week he got better. His juggling especially. Less broken eggs these days.

The eggs dripped from the ceiling into the waiting bowl below. Clumps of flour matted Claude's red hair. She gave him a nod and turned to her work in progress. He always cleaned up his own messes and got his orders done in time. Best to ignore the chaos and get on with her baking. On the wall beside her rested the old

Graham Bakery sign. It covered a hole her cousin put in the wall during his first week.

Mr. Clarke had been Charlotte's grandfather on her mother's side, but Charlotte's father was a Graham. Her parents changed the bakery's name to Graham for all of one week before putting the old sign back up after too much confusion from customers over where Clarke Bakery had gone and one woman who wouldn't stop asking for Mr. Clarke to complain.

She picked up the large mound of dough and turned it over. The dough landed with a plop, sending a dusting of flour over her copy of The String of Pearls. Ever since she started reading about Sweeney Todd, a barber who killed his customers and gave them to Mrs. Lovett for her meat pies, she kept getting distracted by the barber across the street whenever her mind wandered.

The scent of burning bread wafted across her nose. She dropped the dough and yanked the oven door open as fast as she could. Small spots of black dotted two buns in the back of the oven. The rest were a touch too golden, but they would be fine. Besides, she didn't have time to do another batch, not until she finished the rest of the order for the Steepes.

This batch finished off the rolls, but she needed to get the tarts in the oven before the maid arrived to pick up the order. She eyed up the small black spots and checked the timer to make sure she hadn't left the rolls in too long, but no. Five minutes were left. Not a good sign. She popped the lemon tarts into the oven and then kneeled in front of it. The floor creaked beneath her as the heat of the oven drifted over her face. Sweat beaded on her forehead.

The oven was a behemoth, and it wasn't the only one in the kitchen either. They needed several to keep up with the demands of the bakery. Most of the surrounding neighborhoods relied on them for their daily bread. She'd have to remember to check the other ovens later.

Why her grandfather chose to put the runes at the bottom of the oven was beyond her. She'd rather have them somewhere near the top where she wouldn't have to get on the floor to renew them. The etched runes had grown rounded and worn from all the fingers tracing them over the years. The magic of the runes would not only keep the baked goods from burning, but the magic would cook them at the perfect temperature. Assuming the runes were properly tended to. No glow remained in the runes smudged with coal ash and flour. No wonder her buns had burned. The magic had run out.

She sucked in a deep breath and let it out before getting started. As a child her father always treated the runes like the most important tool in their shop and a beloved treasure. Back then he wouldn't let anyone else touch them. The knowledge had been handed down from her grandfather, their own magical family heirloom. On her twelfth birthday he taught Charlotte, but after all these years they no longer felt impressive. Still, she felt the pressure of doing them right even if they'd become another chore to be done instead of something to marvel at, like sweeping the floor or preparing dough for the next morning.

She recited the words her father taught her as her finger traced the etching. According to him they were Latin, but she didn't know any Latin to know if it was true. The mystery of the words went stale ages ago. Her older cousin might understand the words thanks to his Latin classes at university and his lack of being cursed unlike his younger brother, but if he came home her mother would send her to parade around at parties with him. Parties always had the best food, but she was awful at pretending to care about politics and other current events. And her flirting attempts left much to be desired. Husband hunting was far more difficult than baking the perfect loaf of bread.

She finished the spell and the runes shimmered as the magic settled into them. Then the etching turned fiery red, chasing away any doubts of the spell working. The glow gave the impression of hot coals from the shifting magic across the runes. Beautiful, but they'd long become as ordinary in the bakery as the dozens of loafs they churned out every day.

She straightened, blowing a stray strand of dark hair out of her face. She settled onto the stool, eying The String of Pearls with longing. If she started reading now she might miss the timer like last week and everything would dry out. With no time left to remake the tarts, best not to chance it. She'd have to wait to find out the ending she'd been putting off.

All the rejections coming in the mail lately had made her loathe the book. But each time she picked it up, the pages sucked her right back in. Her mind relished the flow of the story and the gruesome imagery. Her story was too similar. Into the Oven followed a wife who, fed up with her alcoholic husband, finally tossed him into the oven to save their bakery. She did the same to the gossipy neighbor who wouldn't stop poking around the bakery. And the man who tried to marry her to take the bakery for himself. None of them survived the oven, and no publisher wanted to serialize the story.

The tinkling of the bell alerted her to a customer.

"Good evening," Laoise's voice called, sounding perfectly prim and proper. "I'm here to pick up the order for tomorrow's party if you please, Mrs. Graham." Her voice brought a smile to Charlotte's face. A visit from Laoise always meant a break. And if she was lucky, scandalous gossip that would offend more delicate ears at parties.

"Of course, Laoise. You can check with Lottie in the back. And tell her to give you a cinnamon bun when you're back there."

"Thank you."

Laoise stepped into the kitchen, her gaze bouncing around before stopping on Charlotte. "Where's your Da?" Like Charlotte's mother, Laoise had red hair that showed off her Irish roots. Charlotte had inherited her father's dark hair, but as a child, she used to stare into the mirror and wonder how she'd look with her mother's hair instead. Nothing against her father, but she'd always thought of it as the boring hair that didn't turn men's heads like Laoise's. Even Laoise's freckles were charming and cute, no matter how many times she complained about them. Being constantly dusted with flour made Charlotte feel like she couldn't compare.

"He's out getting our order of flour."

"And the cinnamon buns? Your Ma said to give me one." Laoise stalked up to the counter like a hungry wolf on the hunt, dropping a stack of baskets down.

Charlotte held out the bun. "Only one left today. I thought you might be by, so I saved it."

Laoise bit into the bun, her eyes rolling up. "Feckin' hell, I swear your bakery makes the best breads. If your Ma ever gets tired of your Da let me know, and I'll marry him meself."

"You'd better hope my mother doesn't hear you talking like that or she will kick you out and you'll never get another free bun." The laugh she held in took the bite out of the threat.

Laoise grinned, her dimples making her look more innocent than she'd ever been. Charlotte would know. The only trouble she got into growing up was whatever trouble Laoise dragged her into.

"One of these days you are going to slip up and my mother will realize you aren't so proper after all."

"She should already know based on what a terror I was as a child." Nothing could match the time Laoise dropped a whole fish into her father's soup as punishment for his bad temper. In comparison Charlotte's father had been too mild mannered and quiet to earn Laoise's ire. "Anyway, I brought you a gift too." She dangled an envelope from between her thumb and pointer finger.

"A letter?"

"No, an invitation."

Charlotte wrinkled her nose. "A luncheon?"

"Better than a luncheon. It's for the tea party! I got you the invitation meself. The Steepes came back from their country estate early this year to host a party before the social season starts. I guess Mr. Steepe wanted first choice of the eligible beauties this year."

Charlotte stared at her, unblinking. "An invitation to a Steepe event? That isn't a funny joke." Laoise had worked for the Steepes for several years now, enough to fill her with stories about their influence and exhausting parties. The Steepes weren't nobility, but they were wealthy thanks to their business dealings that put them as high as a family could go without title.

Laoise scowled. "It's not a joke. I delivered Mr. Steepe a cup of tea right before I left. He asked about the party preparations, and I told him I was about to fetch the bakery order. He complimented your bakery and said it's his favorite. I asked him if he knew the baker had an available daughter."

"You didn't." Charlotte's voice rose a notch in a panic. The luncheons with other small business families had been bad enough, but a party that would have nobility at it? She'd be far too out of place. Her clothing wouldn't be up to their standards or her manners. She'd do nothing but embarrass herself. "He knows I'm a baker too, right?"

Laoise sucked in a breath before continuing as fast as she could speak. "He said he wasn't aware the baker had an available daughter, and that he would send an invitation with me since it was the polite thing to do. I said any man would be lucky to have a wife good at baking and he agreed! He asked me to wait while he fetched another invitation and here it is." She shoved the envelope at Charlotte.

Charlotte eyed it dubiously. "I don't understand why you think I should attend."

"He is looking for a wife! Everyone expects him to choose someone soon." She waggled her eyebrows. "He could choose you if you go."

Charlotte laughed. When Laoise glared she stopped. "Are you being serious?"

"Going won't hurt you. Steepe parties are one of the most sought after invitations in the city, and I got you one."

Charlotte sniffed at the fancy writing on the envelope. Even the elegant loops felt too far above her. "He isn't going to settle for a baker's daughter when his family's reputation could land him a noble's daughter." She got to work packing up the last of the order for the party.

"That isn't the point!" Laoise said through a mouthful of pastry. "The point is to help you make friends who happen to have handsome, single brothers or cousins."

"You sound like my mother."

Laoise shoved the rest of the bun into her mouth and then grabbed Charlotte by the shoulders, forcing her to stop. Charlotte raised her eyebrows, waiting for her friend to finish chewing. "Even Queen Victoria had to marry. The rest of us are no exception. The Steepes have connections to countless other businesses. You could meet a man who could help run the bakery once its yours."

Charlotte folded in on herself. To have to marry to keep the bakery wasn't fair. But the laugh her father's solicitor gave her had been enough to tell her she'd have a battle on her hands. Her mother had her husband at her side when she inherited. Help would be nice when her time came. She could admit that much.

"There, there," Laoise said as she pulled Charlotte into a hug, patting her back hard enough it almost hurt. "On the bright side, without all this baking, you'll have time to write more books." Laoise pulled away to grab the book on the table. She waved it in the air. "You can murder a rich businessman with a baguette or something in the next one. Who dies in this one?" She squinted at the cover.

With a sigh Charlotte pulled her book away. "They don't all have murder in them. And you know all my attempts to get published have failed. Bakeries don't make for chilling enough settings anymore. I need to think of something else." Her notebook full of ideas sat nearby, full of nothing but new recipes and crossed out book ideas.

"A recipe book then for bread." Laosie bumped into the basket of tarts. "Oh, right. The party." Her smile fell. "If I don't get back soon the housekeeper will have my head." She grabbed up as much as she could, hardly making a dent in the pile of baked goods. "Make sure you wear something flattering. Maybe something blue or that lavender dress."

"You do realize the lavender is the only dress I have suitable enough for a party like that?"

"All the easier to choose!" Laoise said, far too cheerful, as she backed out of the kitchen. "I'm going to get the coachman to come grab the rest."

"What was that about a party?" Charlotte's mother asked as she arranged the window display.

Charlotte glared at Laoise, begging with her eyes to not say a word.

Laoise flashed her a demure smile. "Mr. Steepe and his mother sent an invitation for their party tomorrow. Can you help Charlotte with her hair in the morning?"

Charlotte's mother clapped her hands together in delight. "Oh how wonderful!" Her brow furrowed, her smile turning to a frown. "But your dresses won't do for such an occasion. We need to go shopping. And wipe that flour off your cheek."

She dabbed at Charlotte's cheek with her apron. Charlotte wiggled away, knowing she was trapped. Somewhere behind her Laoise complimented the coachman's muscles, offering to get the door for him on his way out. By the time Charlotte pulled on her cloak and took off her apron, Laoise guided the coachman to the door, the basket he carried piled so high with tarts and pies he couldn't see over them.

The gray clouds outside suited Charlotte's mood perfectly. Across the street a new man sat in the barber's chair. His black suit looked perfect. A man that well dressed was probably ready for a party at a moment's notice. He also wouldn't be tempted to wish the barber was Mr. Todd himself if it meant avoiding a party he would be the laughingstock of. Charlotte knew all too well how that felt.

The last party she attended had been six months ago, a luncheon at the Hammond's town house. When some of their dachshunds got loose, the chaos ended with Charlotte leaving in tears and her dress ruined. The hostess blamed her for ruining the party instead of the dogs. The blue dress had been Charlotte's favorite too.

She snagged Laoise's arm as she held the door open for the last haul of sweets. "Please tell me there won't be any dogs."

"I should really get back," Laoise said as she pulled on her gloves and headed out the door.

"Laoise," Charlotte hissed.

Laoise waved. "See you tomorrow! Tell your Da I said 'Hello.'"

"There'd better not be a dog." She balled her hands. "If there is then God help me, I'll cut you off from the pastries."

Laoise gave her one last energetic wave.

Chapter 2

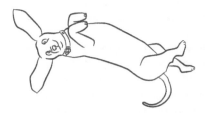

The pale blue of Charlotte's dress flattered the dark curls framing her face. Curls her mother spent an hour making perfect as well as the bun at the back of her head. Extra petticoats and a crinoline added a fashionable volume to her skirt. She couldn't remember the last time she felt this pretty. Being covered in flour tended to make her feel a mess, but in a way that felt familiar. Safe even. But it felt nice to have a reason to dress up again. She wouldn't tell Laoise that though lest it encourage more invitations to parties Charlotte didn't belong at. Laoise really was good at causing trouble.

The cost of the dress weighed on her mind. Could they afford to buy her new dresses to keep up with husband hunting? If she got more invitations she couldn't wear the same dress to every party. Bitter gossips would love preying on her embarrassment. Although invitations had been far and few between since the Hammond's dachshunds got her.

The ride to the Steepe's gave her stomach plenty of time to twist and turn and imagine all the ways she could embarrass herself. Her dress didn't feel lavish enough. And she should have bought new shoes too. Or a chaperone. Didn't the nobility still insist on those?

The stately house didn't help. She gawked at it and the garden sprawling around the front and side yard leaving no room for anything else. She wished she'd paid closer attention to Laoise's stories about the home and family. Most of the gossip had been centered around the servants and entitled, demanding guests. She searched her memory of the stories for any mentions of Mr. Steepe and came up blank. All she could remember was the butler was a strict man and a scullery maid had a crush on him, but she didn't think knowing that would help her today.

She clutched the invitation in her sweating hand, crumpling the paper. The young ladies arriving ahead of her had an older woman for a chaperone. She should have brought her own chaperone, but the bakery couldn't spare both her and her mother. And with Laoise working, she had no choice but to arrive alone. She took a deep breath for courage before knocking, hoping there'd be magicians at this party. They liked to flaunt forgoing such expectations.

The butler answered the door. "Party's been moved to the garden, miss," he said as he pointed to the side of the house. His eyes were glazed with exhaustion in the same way Laoise's often were after working one of the Steepe's parties.

"To the garden? In February?" No dark clouds floated on the horizon, but a frosty chill clung to the air and a recent coating of melting snow crunched underfoot. Luckily she'd borrowed a warm shawl from her mother, but really, a garden party in February? The day was unseasonably warm, but not what she would consider garden party warm.

He shrugged. "Mr. Steepe requested the garden personally. Follow the path. The maids will tend to you in the garden." He pointed at the stepping stones leading to the garden before turning to the next arriving guests, two young ladies with their mothers chaperoning.

She followed the path around the side of the house. As she moved from the front of the house to the side, the garden went from dead plants and empty flower beds to colorful blooms. Despite the season, half of the garden bloomed as bright as a spring day from azalea bushes to roses. A stone fireplace sat on the edge of the grassy expanse in the middle of the garden dotted with trees. A magical net of shimmering gold covered the grassy area, the net winding around the trees and over the fireplace. Inside plants created a riot of color.

She stopped gawking and followed the path closer to the fireplace, magic skittering over her skin as she passed inside the gold net. Goose bumps rose up her arms. Then a wall of warmth from the fire hit her. A magical greenhouse. She'd heard of them, but had never seen one before.

Four round tables sat in the center of the garden in a row. In the center of each table rested tiered trays piled high with sandwiches and tea snacks. If the seats at the table were correct, there would be at least twenty guests. Charlotte guessed that meant twenty guests she wouldn't know.

The nobility had already claimed the table closest to the fireplace as theirs. The other guests couldn't compete with the luxurious silks of their dresses, or get too close to their table without being chased off by cold sneers and upturned noses. One young lady's mother spent much of her time scowling at the table next to them full of what appeared to be magicians' daughters based on the magic they wore like glimmering jewels and star light.

Not unsurprising. Magic used to be a gentleman's pursuit reserved for the nobility until the rise of industrialization drove magic along with it as lower classes got a hold of both magic and new technology. It was becoming more and more common for talented magicians to use magic to gain wealth and influence whether through business or entertainment. They mixed the classes more than the nobility liked. And they had tossed away many social norms the nobility clung to, causing plenty of scandal and irritation.

Like arming their women with magic instead of chaperones. Not to mention their fighting for better working conditions and equality among the classes further deepened the frustration the nobility felt toward them. On the other hand, quite a few popular magicians were beloved by the common people no matter how wild they acted. If anything, their antics endeared them to their loving audiences

Charlotte's attention stopped on the woman standing beside the fountain at the far end of the greenhouse. Her modest dress hinted she wasn't nobility, but rather closer in standing to Charlotte. Something about the woman struck her as familiar, but she couldn't place her. Had they met at another party? Was she a customer? No, that didn't feel right. She knew her from somewhere else, but where?

She snapped her fingers as the answer hit her. The woman was her father's solicitor's daughter. They'd only met a few times, but the woman had always been courteous and talked mostly about flower arranging each time. Charlotte started toward the woman, not wanting to be the guest standing alone the whole party even if she had to spend it discussing the merits of lilies versus roses the whole time. The woman turned to her, her eyebrows rising expectantly.

Charlotte cleared her throat. "Excuse me, how are you? I'm Charlotte Graham."

"How lovely," the woman said, the tone sounding rehearsed. "I'm Mary Hawke."

Oh. Oh no. She was certain the solicitor's daughter's name was Irene. She pressed her sweaty hands against her skirt and swallowed the lump in her throat. "I'm sorry. I mistook you for someone else." Then the name sank in and her eyes widened. "Is that Hawke as in Hawke House?" Hawke Publishing House published many of the popular penny bloods Charlotte read each week. They had a penchant for publishing stories that included monsters and magic with a healthy dose of adventure.

Surprise flitted across Mary's face. "You know of it? Have you read any of Hawke's penny bloods?"

Charlotte's face flamed. Her mother had given her a strict rule on not discussing penny bloods at parties. The one time she brought them up she scandalized another girl who called Charlotte's reading habits uncouth. Apparently murders and highwaymen, whether real or imagined, were too gruesome a topic for polite conversation. "I'm afraid not. I've never read anything that terrifying and tantalizing."

"Me neither," Mary said, her fingers fiddling with her shawl. She rushed on. "We published a cookbook recently that was quite good. I'm fond of the Beef Wellington recipe."

"Are any of the recipes about bread or desserts? My father runs a bakery and I love finding new recipes."

Mary's eyes lit up. "You should come over for tea some time, and I can get you copies of our cookbooks. I'd love to hear some baking tips from you. We usually get our bread from the closest bakery, but I've been trying to make my own. I can never seem to get it to rise right."

This was familiar territory that put Charlotte at ease. There were few topics she knew more about than bread. "That's a common problem and could be due to a few reasons depending on your ingredients. Do you use yeast?"

"Yes. Is that bad?"

"No, but I would start by testing it with warm water and some sugar to make sure it hasn't gone bad. If you've had it sitting around a while it may not rise properly. It's a common issue."

Mary blinked. "Huh, that seems easy enough. I can't remember when I bought it. I'll try that and see if I need new yeast."

"If that doesn't work let me know, and I can take a look."

At the table behind them, all the heads turned at once to look toward the house.

"Presenting, Mrs. Steepe and Mr. Bertram Steepe," a voice boomed out over the garden. The butler trotted ahead of the Steepes with a tea cart filled to the brim with tins of tea. Judging by how young the man escorting Mrs. Steepe was, Charlotte assumed he must be the bachelor in question. He was handsome. No, handsome wasn't enough to do his dashing looks justice. He looked as though he could have been chiseled from marble to become every woman's dream from his strong jawline to his smile that made Charlotte's chest flutter. His perfectly tailored suit complemented his tall, slender frame.

"Come sit with me." Mary linked their arms together in a way that reminded Charlotte of an excited puppy. She suddenly felt silly for being afraid of the party and grateful for Mary's welcome. Mary led the way to the table closest to the fountain. Another young lady already sat at the table, piling sweets onto her plate. She was younger than Charlotte and Mary. Around twenty Charlotte guessed.

"Better sit down before you miss the tea," the woman said. "The table over there was discussing something about a magical teapot being used." She pointed at the table full of women dripping with decorative magic.

Mary gestured to Charlotte. "Margaret, this is Charlotte. She is giving me baking tips on how to make better bread. Charlotte, this is my sister."

"How quaint," Margaret said in the same tone Mary used for 'how lovely,' her attention not leaving the food. "I don't know if anyone can save her bread. The last loaf didn't even look like bread." Then she bit into a tart, her eyes fluttering in delight.

"At least I tried. Do you think Mr. Steepe is going to choose a fiancée soon after all?" Mary whispered as she sat down beside Margaret.

"Not like it is going to be us. I'm here for the food."

Charlotte found the sentiment all too easy to agree with. "Why can't it be either of you?"

"We're only here because Mr. Steepe has done business with our father. He's never met us. I didn't think he knew we existed until we received the invitation."

"But this is so wonderful!" Mary gushed. "Look at how pretty the garden is and all the food. This is the perfect way to spend a beautiful day outside." She gave them a dreamy sigh as she clasped her hands to her chest. Unlike the table of nobility who wore light shawls that weren't suited to the weather, Mary and Margaret had dressed more sensibly in heavier shawls and dresses.

"Forgive my sister," Margaret said as she finally looked at Charlotte. "She loves parties, and we've never been invited to a Steepe fête before. It could snow and she wouldn't care. And maybe it will, being February and all."

"I haven't either." What an odd party, Charlotte thought, with its strange mix of women. The tables had filled since she arrived and everyone stuck to whichever table they'd chosen, less out of suspicion of the other tables she thought, and more to stay near the hot tea for warmth.

"Is anyone sitting here?" A young lady in a royal purple dress asked as she stood behind the empty seat next to Charlotte, her mouth twisted in distaste. The dress matched the latest fashion despite its faded fabric. The woman was tall with a willowy figure that made her look delicate despite her tall height.

"Elizabeth," Margaret greeted in a frosty tone, her eyes narrowing.

"No one is," Mary said, the dreamy tone lingering in her voice.

Elizabeth lowered herself into the chair, saying nothing as she helped herself to the food while Margaret frowned at her.

Charlotte leaned toward Mary. "Erm, who is she?"

"She's Elizabeth Holloway, daughter of Baron Holloway."

Elizabeth stuck her chin in the air. "What are you? An accountant's daughter? A tailor's daughter?" She peered down her nose at Charlotte.

"A baker's daughter actually."

Elizabeth's expression froze as if she wasn't sure whether or not to believe her. "Is that a joke?"

"No. My bakery made many of the sweets for this party."

"Clarke Bakery?" Margaret said, waving a tart in the air. "They are one of the best bakeries in the city."

"Was there a mix up with the invitations?" Elizabeth's nose wrinkled. "Or did you deliver the food and then sneak in? Someone should tell the butler you are here."

"Ignore her," Margaret said, flapping a hand. "She is always rude to those she sees as beneath her. Don't waste your time on her." Her attention caught on something over Mary's shoulder, and she got to work wiping the crumbs off the table in a hurry. "Mrs. Steepe is coming."

"Don't forget your face." Mary shoved a napkin into Margaret's hand. "The right corner of your mouth." She pointed at her own face to clarify.

Margaret dabbed at her face, getting the crumb sticking to the side of her mouth.

Mrs. Steepe strolled up to their table, the butler following with the tea cart.

"Ladies, thank you all for coming," Mrs. Steepe said, her warm voice inviting despite the frosty looks being shot at their table from the nobles. She wore a flattering blue and yellow dress with a simple teardrop sapphire necklace at her throat. "I hope you enjoy the food and tea."

Mr. Steepe stepped up beside her, his outfit equally as fashionable. His dark frock coat accentuated his lean silhouette. His top hat added height to his already tall frame.

"The butler will be by soon to pour your tea. The maids will be bringing out more shortly as well. Please let them know if you need anything." His deep voice rang through Charlotte. If she hadn't already been as straight as her corset demanded, that rich voice would have made her straighten up. Seeing him up close made her mind swim as she struggled to think clearly. When he turned his chocolate brown eyes on her, Charlotte worried she would melt on the spot.

If this was Mr. Steepe, no wonder the women at the party wanted to be chosen as his bride. Forget securing invitations to other parties, she'd rather spend all day staring into his eyes and listening to his smooth voice.

"Please enjoy yourselves," he said, giving them one all last smile before turning away and heading back to the table of nobles calling to him.

"Stop gawking," Elizabeth chided.

Charlotte blushed, hoping Mr. Steepe hadn't noticed. "He's rather handsome, isn't he?"

Mary and Margaret both giggled, the sound identical.

"I take it you think he is," Mary said. "He's known for his handsome looks. He is why all the available women long to be invited to the Steepes' parties."

Elizabeth rolled her eyes. "A man needs more than good looks to be worth marrying."

The butler stepped up to the table with a tea cart. "Good afternoon, ladies," he said. "I will be using a teapot engraved with runes today if you'll please listen to my instructions to ensure the magic works properly." He paused, making sure he had their attention. "You will each need to touch your teacups with your hands, sans gloves please. Then I will pour your tea."

In unison they all reached for their cups. Then he began pouring, starting with Mary. Hot water poured into her cup, steam wafting off it. Mary frowned in confusion. Just as she opened her mouth to protest the water darkened and the citrus tang of an Earl Grey wafted off her cup. Her eyes widened in surprise. The butler moved on to Margaret, making his way around the table to end with Charlotte. She watched in wonder as the water in her cup darkened. She breathed in the smoky scent of Lapsang Souchong, the smell comforting her and reminding her of nights gathered around the fireplace with her family.

"Excuse me," Elizabeth said, making a face at her tea. "But mine is nothing but hot water."

The butler leaned over to peer into her cup. A few seconds later the cup remained nothing but hot water. "Ah, yes. You must prefer coffee."

Elizabeth's head lifted toward him in surprise. "I do."

"How unfortunate," he said as he reached for the pot of coffee sitting behind the teapot and poured her a mug of it.

Elizabeth spluttered in indignation, unable to get any words out before he walked away. "How rude!" she finally huffed.

"Did we all get a different tea?" Mary sniffed at Charlotte's cup, her nose wrinkling. "Margaret, what did you get?"

"I don't have any inkling." Margaret took a sip, her face lighting up. "But it tastes heavenly. I would ask you what you got, Elizabeth, except you didn't get any tea. And at a tea party no less!"

Elizabeth sneered. "I don't care what you think about my beverage choices." She lifted her mug of coffee to her lips.

Mary ignored her and took another sip of her tea. "I detect a hint of hazelnut in mine. I like it."

Charlotte's eyes followed Mr. Steepe as he roved about the greenhouse.

Elizabeth pointed an accusing finger at Charlotte. "Stop staring at Mr. Steepe! You don't have a chance with this family. Everyone knows they are trying to marry into nobility."

"If they go for a noble's daughter, I'm certain they will go higher than the daughter of a baron who is up to his eyeballs in gambling debts." Margaret smiled at a magician's daughter who wandered past the table as though she weren't in the middle of hurling insults across the table.

Elizabeth's face reddened. She lowered her mug, her gaze catching on the tray of food. Then she dumped her coffee all over the top tray. The liquid trickled over the side and onto the sandwiches below. "Oops, how clumsy of me." She lifted a hand to her heart, her mouth twitching as she suppressed her smile.

Mary gasped. Margaret pulled the bottom tray of pastries away from the stand before the coffee dripping over the sides of the top tray could reach it. "You ruined our food!"

The women at the next table over turned to stare. Charlotte squeezed her teacup. This was not how she wanted the party to go. Heat creeped up her neck as the women continued to watch their drama play out. This felt too much like the Hammond Luncheon, but without all the laughter aimed her way.

"Good day to you all." Elizabeth stood, sticking her nose high in the air, and headed for the table of magicians. When one saw her coming, she tossed her shawl onto the free chair. Elizabeth made a sharp right turn and headed out of the garden. Their audience turned back to their food and drinks.

Mary patted Charlotte's hand. "Don't mind what she said. She always has a sharp tongue. She gets into arguments at every party she attends."

"I wish she wouldn't have ruined our food," Margaret said.

"We can ask a maid or the butler for more." Mary twisted this way and that, trying to find an available maid. The butler was busy refilling teacups and Laoise and the other maid were running this way and that taking care of requests for the first two tables.

"I-I'll be back." Charlotte shot out of her chair. She headed around the large fountain, just out of sight of the tables thanks to the large bushes blocking the view. She took several deep breaths to calm herself. There were no dogs, she reminded herself. She could survive a mere tea party, even if it was outside in February. The heat of the bakery's kitchen would feel that much better when she returned home.

"You'd better not be hiding," a voice hissed, making her jump. Laoise.

"It got scary. I needed to escape."

"Scary? It's a tea party."

"A tea party full of women ready to tear each other apart for a piece of Mr. Steepe."

"Find your confidence. Or fake it, but I can't let you hide here when I got you an invitation. I might not be able to get you another. Don't waste this one."

She was right and Charlotte didn't want to let her down. "How about this?" She wiped the terror off her face and threw her shoulders back.

"Your eyes are too wide, but close enough. Remember you are beautiful and make the best bread in the whole city. Anyone who doesn't see how great you are is a fool. Now go!" Laoise pushed her back toward the tables. A noble rang for a maid and Laoise rushed off, leaving Charlotte wishing she'd thought to ask for fresh food. If she was going to fake confidence and stay, she'd rather do it on a full stomach.

Confidence, she reminded herself as she strolled up to the kitchen. It wasn't far, but when she reached it she found it a whirlwind of chaos. The heat of the kitchen hit her like a wall, reminding her of the bakery. This was the kind of heat that made the winter cold harder to bear, but it kept the inside of the bakery cozy. A haze of steam and smoke hung in the air. No maid stopped long enough for her to get a word out as they rushed all about with trays and dishes. Someone shouted for more hot water. She spotted a maid rushing past with a tray of dirty teacups.

"Exc—" Charlotte stopped as the maid continued past, not sparing her a single glance. The maid set the tray down on a counter piled with dishes. Down the counter the butler stood with his back to her, pouring hot water into the teapot that had been used earlier to pour their tea. He murmured under his breath and she assumed he was speaking to the runes. She waited a minute until he stopped, squinting through the hazy air at him.

"Um, excuse me, but our food got coffee spilled on it. Can we get a new sandwich platter?" The heavenly smells of the kitchen made her stomach ache with hunger. Garlic and sage danced through the air. "The food looked good, but I don't want to be a bother if there is nothing left." Off by the stove something sizzled, the scent of beef joining the spices.

"Of course, miss. Which table?" He looked over his shoulder at her.

"The one closest to the side entrance to the garden, please."

"I'll have some sent out immediately."

"Thank you very much. Excellent tea today," she added, feeling like she should say more in thanks. A maid rushed by with the tea cart, missing Charlotte's foot by a hand width. She backed out of the kitchen before someone else tried to run her foot over. Despite the danger, she'd done it. Maybe Laoise was right, a little more confidence went a long way. She stepped onto the main garden path leading back to the tables and found Mr. Steepe coming her way. She put on a smile, heart hammering in her chest.

"Mr. Steepe, lovely party."

"My aunt spares no expense for her son," he said, giving her his charming smile,

"Her son?" Her thoughts sputtered as she tried to make sense of the connection. "That is to say...not you?"

"Oh no, that would be my cousin, Martin. I'm Bertram Steepe. I know it can get confusing when everyone calls us both Mr. Steepe. People mix us up all the time."

The handsome cousin. The one Laoise had far too many stories about. She really should have tried to remember more details from those stories. If this Mr. Steepe was the handsome cousin everyone wanted, then who was the Mr. Steepe looking for a bride?

He looked past her at the house. "I'm off to find him actually. Sometimes he gets caught up discussing magic with his butler." A frown tugged on his lips.

"I don't want to keep you then." She smiled through her disappointment. She made for her table, telling herself it should have been obvious the handsomest man in Great Britain didn't need a party to find a bride. A man like him would have plenty of choices.

"More food will be here soon," she informed Mary and Margaret. Margaret snacked on one of the pastries she managed to save from Elizabeth's wrath.

"Thank goodness," Margaret said. She stared sullenly at the table of nobles. "Two of the women over there have already asked for at least three different cups of tea, unable to be satisfied with anything. The maids can't escape."

Laoise looked harried with hair beginning to fall from her bun as she set a fresh pot of tea onto the nobles' table. One of the women snapped her fingers as if Laoise was a dog and it made Charlotte wish someone would spit in her drink. A minute later a maid appeared with a new tray of food. Margaret clapped her hands in delight at the sight, wasting no time on digging in.

"I want one of every flavor of cheese and sandwich," she announced as she piled little sandwich triangles onto her plate. I've heard their cook is amazing."

"There he is!" Mary said, fanning herself. Margaret continued digging into the food.

"Presenting Mr. Martin Steepe," the butler called out.

Charlotte turned. Her stomach dropped, and she pressed a hand to her mouth to suppress the embarrassment and horror threatening to boil over at the sight of the man. He wasn't as tall as his cousin, but his suit was just as fine and stylish. Unlike in the kitchen, he wore his top hat this time. She hadn't asked the butler for food. No, she'd asked Mr. Martin Steepe. Worse he was heading for their table. Her face burned. "I-I need to go."

"Charlotte!" Mary called as Charlotte dashed away from the table, her shawl falling off in her haste.

A few steps later she realized she'd lost the shawl. No, not her shawl, it was her mother's. Her favorite one too. Guilt assailed her at the thought of returning without it. She turned and marched back to the table, hesitating when she saw Martin was already there. What must he think of her mistaking him for the butler? There was no good way to talk herself out of the situation. This could become worse than the Hammond Luncheon.

"I hope the food is satisfactory ladies," he said to Mary and Margaret.

Mary giggled. "It is perfect, Mr. Steepe."

He smiled, looking as though he didn't fully hear her as his gaze roved over their empty teacups. "Whose cup is that?" he asked, pointing to Charlotte's.

"It's hers," Margaret said as Charlotte grabbed her shawl off her chair.

"Wonderful party," Charlotte said, her stomach clenching from nerves. "But I should be going. Good day." She stepped back, turning to rush off and drown her woes in freshly baked bread at home.

"Wait!" Martin called, stepping around the table to intercept her.

"This is your cup, isn't it?" He snatched it off the table and held it up, inspecting the empty cup. Good heavens had she ruined the cup or something? Charlotte's mind swam as there seemed to be no end to her embarassment. He set the cup down, his eyes wild as he leaned toward her. Her vision tunneled until she saw nothing but his face. Her palms sweat and her heart roared in her ears.

She realized he was talking, but she didn't catch a single word. He had to be mad about being mistaken for his butler. What man wouldn't be? He stared at her, waiting for a reply, eagerness in his expression. Mary and Margaret watched them, eyes wide as teacup saucers.

"Yes, I'm so sorry," she blurted out.

He smiled, and she nodded, repeating herself, mortified of what he must think of her mistake.

"Marvelous! Please come with me." He went back to the tea cart, ringing the bell on it. The loud ring from the little silver bell quieted everyone down. Confused faces turned their way, Martin's mother and Bertram included. "Everyone, please allow me to introduce my new fiancée."

One woman choked on her drink, coughing as tea sloshed out of her cup and all over her table.

"Her?" another called in disgust from the table of nobility.

Charlotte froze, refusing to believe she'd heard him correctly. She searched for a way out. All the stares made her feel faint. Ah-ha! That was it exactly, just like that one penny blood she read last month where the woman fainted at the announcement of her beau's elopement to another woman.

And so Charlotte fainted to the tune of gasps, all too happy to put the uncomfortable stares out of sight.

Chapter 3

Or at least she tried to faint. Seeing as how she'd never fainted before, she could do nothing but put on her best performance and hope it worked. She pressed one hand to her forehead and moaned as she went down, mimicking the actress in the last play she saw. She lowered herself to the ground, first falling to her knees and then flopping over, afraid her dress would catch on the nearby bushes if she fell the wrong direction.

"Marty!" Mr. Steepe's mother cried out in horror. "Do something!"

"Did she really just faint?" someone asked. Murmurs answered.

"Too much excitement, the poor thing," Mary said, sympathy filling the words.

Charlotte squeezed her eyes shut, fighting the urge to open them and see what was happening. Even without seeing she could feel all the eyes boring into her. The faint didn't feel like enough to make them stop. If anything it'd made the attention worse.

"Perhaps you should take her inside?" Bless Mary, she was the angel Charlotte needed. Inside would be the perfect escape from the stares.

"Yes, Marty, take her inside," his mother urged.

"If you think that would be best," Mr. Steepe replied.

Charlotte bit her tongue to hold in her yelp as someone suddenly lifted her off the ground. Mr. Steepe she assumed, but she didn't dare peek to find out. The light citrus note wafting from him reminded her of Earl Grey tea.

"Not you! Let the butler carry her," his mother fretted. "You'll over tax yourself."

"Nonsense, I haven't been sick in years. I can handle carrying her inside." He readjusted his grip, and it sent her stomach plummeting. She silently begged him to not drop her. He started walking and the bouncing made her stomach swoop. It would be a new record of family scandal disgracing herself with the Steepe family. She'd eclipse her uncle who fell in love with an actress who, unbeknownst to him, was already pregnant with another man's child. She could write her downfall into a penny blood and let everyone laugh at her misfortune. In the novel version, he'd definitely drop her. Right into the fountain.

He laid her down on a chaise lounge with gentle care. Except her arm dangled over one edge, the uncomfortable position threatening to put her arm to sleep.

"Should we call a doctor?" he asked, concern ringing clear in his voice. "I do hope she didn't hit her head."

A doctor would know she was faking it. There'd no graceful way to admit the truth, but how to get out of this in a way that wasn't suspicious? Would anyone think to pull out smelling salts first?

"Maybe you ought to try tickling her, Mr. Steepe." Laoise. Damn her, Charlotte would kill her when all this was over. Laoise coughed, hiding a laugh.

"Is ... is that what you are supposed to do when a lady faints?"

"Easier than getting a doctor."

Heels tapped across the floor and Laoise went silent. "Has she not woken yet? Perhaps we should send for our doctor. Who is she, Marty?"

"She is my fiancée."

A long, withering sigh came from his mother. "I meant her name. What is her name?"

"Oh, of course. She is Miss ..." The silence stretched out. The muscle in Charlotte's arm started to cramp. She gritted her teeth against the pain. "I'm afraid I forgot in my excitement."

Had he asked? Charlotte couldn't remember a word he'd said, and she doubted anyone would mistake "yes, I'm sorry" as a name.

"But she was the only one who chose Lapsang Souchong and that my spell deemed a good match."

His mother let out a sigh that somehow managed to be even longer than the first. "You'd better find out her name if you plan on explaining this to your father when he gets back from his business trip. I'm going to go see to our guests. Call for the doctor if she doesn't wake soon. We'll discuss this later. In private." She left, the tapping of her heels fading away.

A choking noise came from Laoise followed by a hiccup.

"Don't cry!" Mr. Steepe said, panic finally entering his voice. "I'm sure the lady will be fine ... Oh dear, if she isn't do you think she'll call off the engagement?"

Laoise wheezed in response.

A new tapping made its way across the floor, this one too quiet to be heels. A slimy tongue flicked across her chin and she squealed. She opened her eyes, finding a light brown dachshund staring back at her, his head cocked to the side. He went in for lick two, but she jerked up to get her face out of range.

"Oolong! No licking." Martin picked up the dog, and it wiggled in excitement, giving Charlotte a look that made her think he would lick her again if given the chance.

"What is that?" Her voice came out shrill. She'd been so afraid of disgrace, she hadn't realized the dachshunds weren't finished with her.

"His name is Oolong." Mr. Steepe held the dog out in front of him and Oolong wiggled again as he tried to throw himself onto Charlotte's lap. Behind them Laoise's shoulders shook as she pressed a hand to her mouth to keep her laughter quiet. "I'm glad you're all right, miss." He tried to bow, but Oolong got in the way, the dog's head bumping into his chin. Mr. Steepe glanced around and spotted Laoise who stood by the wall. He shoved Oolong at her stomach, forcing her to take the dog. Oolong turned his tongue on her, catching her chin before she held him away.

"Martin Steepe at your service." He managed an elegant bow this time.

"Charlotte Graham." She peeked at Laoise, making sure she had a tight grip on Oolong.

"A pleasure, Miss Graham. Is there anything I can get for you? More tea or some sandwiches? Or perhaps a doctor?"

"I'm fine," she said, voice cracking.

"Are you certain? I can fetch you more lapsang if you'd like."

"Rest is all I need." Her dry mouth protested, but more tea meant staying longer. She'd rather make a run for it the first chance she got.

"I'll look after her, Mr. Steepe." Laoise said, the words hoarse.

"That is a great idea," Charlotte said, escape feeling deliciously close at hand. "I need to lie down a bit longer in here where it's quiet."

"All right," he said, taking Oolong back from Laoise as the dog wiggled. "If you change your mind or need anything, let me know. If I might ask before I return to the party, why do you like Lapsang Souchong, Miss Graham?"

The question took her by surprise. She shifted as she considered how to answer. "My father received the tea as a gift one Christmas when I was a child and loved it. He has kept it on hand ever since. He says it is a tea fit for nobility and drinking it makes him feel like a grand duke." She used to pretend to be a princess their first Christmas drinking it, taking his proclamations about the tea seriously. Afterward her father pretended to dance with her at a ball. She hadn't liked the tea back then. She had found the smoky taste too overpowering, but it grew on her over the years. Now the tea was as entwined with her feelings of home and her father as much as the smell of bread was.

"I see." He lingered, and she shot Laoise a pleading look.

"I think she needs peace and quiet, Mr. Steepe. I can fetch her more tea if she wants it."

"Very good," he murmured, finally heading for the door. He glanced back when he reached the door, hesitating. Then he left and Laoise let out a long, wheezing laugh. "The look on your face!"

"It's not funny." Charlotte crossed her arms over her chest.

"You're right. It's hilarious." She clutched her side. "What was that faint? Were you trying to lie down and take a nap?"

Charlotte's cheeks puffed in indignation. "How about I hold you getting me an invitation to this debacle over your head for the rest of our lives?"

"Please do. I never want to forget today. How are you going to explain all this to your parents? Mr. Steepe thinks you are engaged." She giggled. "Did you hear him when he said he'd like to marry you? You kept telling him you were sorry."

Charlotte flushed. "I mistook him for the butler earlier, and I thought that was what he was asking about. I didn't hear a word of what he said to me."

Laoise let go of her side. "The butler? What?"

Charlotte flopped back down. "The spoiled noble woman at our table dumped her coffee on our sandwiches, so I went to the kitchen to ask for more. Mr. Steepe was in there near a pile of teacups. He had his back to me and I mistook him for the butler and asked for more food."

Laoise broke out in a fresh round of giggles, tears leaking from her eyes. "This gets better 'n better. You are lucky it was him and not his cousin. He isn't as forgiving to that sort of thing. He's very strict in fact." Laoise dropped her voice. "Sometimes I worry Mr. Steepe isn't always all there, if you get what I'm saying."

Charlotte's mouth hung open in shock. "Why didn't you warn me?"

"I didn't think he would say more than a polite 'hello' to you. He isn't a bad man, just forgetful and...odd. But rich, and isn't that what matters in the end?"

"Well I'm not rich, which is why it will never work out once he discovers who I am." Charlotte took in the room for the first time.

A painting of the family hung above the fireplace. Mr. Steepe's father looked dour while a wane Martin who couldn't be more than twelve smiled. His mother gripped his shoulder, a melancholy air about her. A thick rug sat in front of the divan. The rest of the room was furnished elegantly without a speck of dust to be seen. "That's twice you've called him odd. Is he that eccentric?"

"He did propose to you based off the tea his enchanted teapot gave you." She arched a brow at Charlotte, daring her to disagree. "Before bothering to ask your name at that."

Charlotte's shoulders slumped. "Good point. All right then, how about you help me sneak out of here? I don't think I have it in me to face all those guests or Mr. Steepe again today." She'd rather curl up in her room or a corner of the bakery with a book and hot tea and bury today's events deep in her mind until she could forget about them. As if that was possible. She'd never forget. Today would haunt her nightmares and plague her thoughts whenever she couldn't sleep.

Laoise ordered a carriage prepared. Together they sneaked out the front door and waited.

"What do you want me to tell him when Mr. Steepe realizes you are gone?"

"Tell him I wasn't feeling well and wanted to go home to lie in bed. Or that I don't marry men who don't know my name. Whichever you think prudent."

Laoise grinned. "I'll tell him you were loath to leave but are eagerly waiting for flowers from him."

"Don't you dare. My mother might faint for real if he sends me flowers. You'll get her hopes up."

"Aye." Laoise gave her a grim nod. "I volunteer to keep your Da company while you look after her."

She gave Laoise's shoulder a light smack. "No! I can't believe he thinks you are such a sweet young lady. He wouldn't be able to handle you."

"I can't help meself. All those muscles from lifting heavy bags of flour and kneading dough are worth swooning over." Laoise pressed her hands against her cheeks. "If I could squeeze them once, I would die happy. Your mother is a lucky lady."

"She'd never let you have him. Neither would I."

"Doesn't mean I can't try."

The Steepe's carriage rolled up. A teenaged boy sat on the driver's bench. Charlotte tightened her hold on the shawl to keep from forgetting it a second time.

"Marcus is a good lad and will see you home. I should get back to the party before Shannon finds a dark corner somewhere to lie down and give up. I should drag Anna out of the kitchen to help us while I'm at it."

"Good luck. And thank you for the carriage. I might be able to forgive you someday."

"Give me a pastry next time I stop by the bakery, and I'll forgive you for not forgiving me sooner." Laoise held the carriage door open for her and gave her a curtsy. "My lady."

Charlotte rolled her eyes. "Let me know if you find out anything about ... all this." She waved her hands at her sides.

"Will do." Laoise stepped back, and the carriage jolted forward. She waved. Charlotte slumped in her seat. The rocking of the carriage tightened her cramping stomach. She would need to figure out a way to explain to her parents. There was no way they'd believe it. She couldn't believe the engagement herself. Her mother would jump to conclusions and ask too many questions. No, she wasn't looking forward to that conversation at all.

First a quick stop at the bookstore wouldn't hurt. It'd give her time to gather her thoughts and find a way to explain. Yes, a good book was exactly what she needed for perspective. Something where someone suffered far worse mortifying moments than her.

Chapter 4

By the time Charlotte woke, the sun was shining outside her window. The light sent her scrambling to get dressed. She must be three hours late for work. It was her fault for staying out until past supper to avoid telling her parents about the party. Her mother hadn't come to wake her, which meant they either had their hands full with the bakery or Laoise somehow told on her. A bang came from below, reminding her of the option she didn't want to consider: her cousin was causing a mess of the bakery again.

She crept down the stairs. In the kitchen, her father's steady voice recited recipes and directions. She nearly bumped into her mother in the doorway to the kitchen, sidestepping in time to avoid knocking the rolls off her tray.

"Finally up? Yesterday must have been exciting. You stayed out late and then went straight to bed." She kept her voice light, but her eyes watched Charlotte like a cat stalking prey.

Charlotte chewed on her bottom lip. Unable to figure out how to explain she'd gone elsewhere, browsing every store she could find and then found a table in a cafe to catch up on her reading to avoid explaining. Best to avoid that admission. "What can I do to help?"

"Your father has everything under control. A new assistant is starting today. Your cousin is a good learner but the curse gets in his way too often. Once the new assistant settles in you won't need to spend your time baking any longer." Her mother tossed the buns into the display case. "How was the party?"

So much for distracting her from the topic. "It was … unusual." No words she could think of could do the party and her sudden engagement justice. Should she consider it a real engagement? Mr. Steepe could have come to his senses by now and realized he shouldn't agree to a woman he knew nothing about other than her taste in tea.

Her mother frowned. "What do you mean by that? Were our baked goods liked?"

"They were. Everyone seemed pleased with the pastries." Margaret especially. Remembering her butler gaffe made her want to go hide under the table. How could she have made that mistake? Her cheeks tingled as she fought down her embarrassment. "The party didn't go as I expected. Nothing about it in fact. The Steepes held the party outside despite the weather. But did you know they have a magical greenhouse? It was rather comfortable I—"

"You're rambling. What are you trying to avoid telling me? Did something happen?"

Leave it to her mother to see through her. "I may have fainted at the end."

Her mother dropped the empty tray. "Fainted? Are you all right?" She grabbed Charlotte by the shoulders, assessing her. She pressed a hand to her forehead, checking her temperature. "You should go see the doctor."

"I'm fine." Charlotte pulled herself free. "It wasn't a real faint."

"What?" Her mother's voice came out shrill. "You faked a faint at a tea party? At the Steepe's house?"

"I had good reason or else I wouldn't have done it. It was worse than the Hammond's luncheon and their dachshunds." She'd burned her blue dress that night. Was it melodramatic? Yes. But there'd been no saving that dress. Not that she'd wanted to. She didn't need any reminders about her humiliation.

Her mother clapped her hands over her ears, making a noise of distress deep in her throat. "Don't talk to me about that dreadful day. I can't bare it. You'd be better off forgetting it ever happened."

"Believe me, I wish I could forget about that day. I wish everyone else would too." She'd go to all the parties she was invited to if she knew no one would bring up the incident or snicker at her behind her back. Unfortunately for her, her invitations were too sparse to make a trade like that. They'd all but fallen off a cliff since the Hammond luncheon. As much as she'd enjoyed the break at first, she'd enjoyed meeting Mary. Spending all day in the bakery kitchen was lonelier than she'd realized. A shame her faint would doom whatever remained of her reputation. It would be a miracle to ever get an invitation again.

The shop's bell dinged, alerting them to customers. She silently cursed the bad timing. Nothing would be a big enough distraction to make her mother forget their conversation. Customers could do nothing but delay the inevitable.

"I'm glad you finally came with me, Bertie." Mr. Steepe's voice made Charlotte's eyes bulge in shock. She glanced over her shoulder, finding Mr. Steepe talking to his cousin who looked about the room in a way that suggested he thought the bakery beneath him. No doubt he was used to having servants handle all his food.

Bertram's gaze headed toward Charlotte, and she dashed for the kitchen. She wasn't ready for this, not here in front of her parents. She thought he'd send a letter, or another invitation for tea first if he figured out where she lived. Then they'd talk about what a wild story it all was while he apologized about his magic going astray or mistaking her for someone else.

"I do love good bread," Bertram said, his voice monotone.

"Good morning," Mr. Steepe called out, his voice warm. "Do you have any more cinnamon buns?"

"We pulled a fresh batch out of the oven five minutes ago," Charlotte's mother answered.

"Wonderful. We'll take two."

"I'll go fetch them." She gave them a smile before heading into the kitchen. "What has gotten into you?" she hissed as she caught Charlotte hiding out of sight.

"That's him! That's Mr. Steepe. I can't let him see me like this." She tugged on her old brown dress. An old tea stain marred the right sleeve. The faded flowers could barely be seen any more on the rough fabric. She'd never wear the dress out. It was one of her work dresses where she hid the stains and patches under her apron. "What would he tell people about me if he saw me like this?" There was already enough gossip after her faint to go around for weeks.

Her mother peered out of the doorway, a smile creeping onto her lips. "Look at his stylish suit and that cleft in his chin. And that strong jawline." She bit her bottom lip. "I bet he is a man who likes to hunt." The admiration in her voice reminded Charlotte too much of the way Laoise spoke of Charlotte's father. It made her squirm. She was also certain her father had never hunted a day in his life.

"What?" Horror dripped from the word. She never knew her mother's tastes outside of her father.

"He's handsome. I bet you couldn't find a more handsome man in all of London if you tried."

"Not him. The other one." She elbowed her mother to stop her from drooling over Bertram.

Her mother's pleased smile fell. "Oh. I suppose you could call him handsome too."

"Remember that bit about me fainting? I fainted because he thinks we're engaged."

Her mother whirled on her. "What?"

Charlotte hushed her. "Like I said, it's a strange story. Point being he can't see me dressed like this." If he hadn't changed his mind about the engagement yet, he was bound to after seeing her in this outfit.

"Quite right." Her mother nodded as she spoke. "What if he asks for you? What should I tell him?"

"I don't think he knows I'm here. He is here for cinnamon buns, not me. And that's why I can't go out there or he'll find out."

Her father moved around the counter to join them as he wiped his hands on a rag. "Did I hear right that you got engaged, Lottie? The man didn't even come ask for my permission first. He'd better be very wealthy."

"He only proposed because he doesn't know I'm a baker's daughter."

"Then who does he think you are? And why didn't you tell me you were interested in courting him?" His forehead wrinkled in concern. "I only want you to find someone who makes you happy." Hurt sharpened the edges of the words. "I'd never throw a bag of flour at him like your grandfather did to me."

A nervous laugh threatened to burst from her. Her father had never been one to discuss marriage with her, but the idea of him throwing a bag of flour at Mr. Steepe unsettled her. "I'll explain everything later!" She thought back on her conversation with Mr. Steepe, and her eyes widened as she considered her story about the lapsang. "I may have accidentally implied we're nobility."

Her father smacked a hand to his face. "As soon as he finds out you're not, he'll call off the engagement. A man of his reputation will want to marry into more money or a noble title. I don't want to see you hurt, Lottie. I can't offer a man like that a high enough dowry."

The rising class of magicians had already done away with money dowries, considering magic enough of a gift. Mr. Steepe knew magic, but she didn't know where his ideals fell. He could be as old-fashioned as the oldest noble families who knew magic.

"Not if he falls in love first!" her mother protested. "This could be a blessing in disguise." Her gaze roved back to the Steepes. "Is his cousin available?"

"I don't think so."

The disappointment on her face was obvious. "Mr. Steepe is a perfectly good choice too. Any man would be lucky to have you, chin cleft or no. I'm sure a man with his business background could appreciate a family business like ours."

Bertram cleared his throat. Loudly. "Excuse me, are the cinnamon buns ready?" Impatience marred his attempt at a polite tone.

"Please go get rid of them," Charlotte hissed in a whisper.

"Fine, but you'd better explain the rest soon." Her mother stepped toward the door. Charlotte yanked her back.

"You forgot the cinnamon buns."

"How forgetful of me," she said, her gaze lingering on Bertram, a hunger to her eyes Charlotte had never seen before.

Charlotte shoved the tray of fresh rolls into her mother's hands. "Go!"

Her mother stepped back into the shop, looking like a love-drunk school girl as she fretted over the Steepes, asking if she could get them anything else and offering a few suggestions.

Her father turned back to kneading a large bowl of dough. "If there has been a misunderstanding, I think you should go pay Mr. Steepe a visit this evening to sort this matter out. And don't get your hopes up no matter what your mother says." He paused, throwing the rag over his shoulder. "I'd marry you to a duke if I could, but our standing isn't in your favor. Don't let him hurt you. There is plenty of time to find a good man for you."

"Yes, Father. I'll go today." What to say to Mr. Steepe wouldn't be an easy matter. What man would take kindly to discovering his noble fiancée was actually a baker's daughter? It made the thought of marching out and revealing herself the easier option if she wasn't afraid of causing a scene in front of other customers.

The bell above the door rang. She peeked around the corner, making sure the Steepes were gone before stepping back out.

"Lottie," her father called.

She glanced back into the kitchen, ignoring the way her cousin Claude caught a bowl of dough as it toppled off the counter. His hand knocked it back onto the counter where the dough rolled out, somehow perfectly shaped.

"If he does want to marry you, you have my blessing as long as that is what you want. Don't go marrying anyone you won't be happy with, and don't let anyone pressure you. Not even your mother."

"Thank you." He'd never been a talkative man, but she'd always counted on him, and he'd never let her down.

As she stepped back into the front room, her mother wagged a finger at her. "I heard Mr. Steepe say he is heading home next. You march up those stairs and put something nicer on. You need to pay him a visit."

"Tell him who you are!" her father called out.

"No!" Her mother grabbed her by the shoulders again. "Don't let him know who you are until he's madly in love with you. Then he won't want to end the engagement."

"I can't do that. I don't know anything about him. Except he likes tea, especially Lapsang Souchong. What basis is that for a marriage?"

Her mother sighed. "Nothing matters with money like his on the table. He can keep you comfortable and safe and that is more than most women could hope for. If he would make you miserable, I understand. But if not, at least give the man a fair chance. You could have your own servants!"

"I will think about it," Charlotte conceded.

"Don't underestimate yourself. Make sure you put on one of your best dresses and wipe that flour off your chin."

Charlotte marched upstairs, mulling over the advice and what to do. She didn't think Mr. Steepe would make her miserable, but she didn't know anything about him at all to be able to say. But tea as a basis for a marriage? The peculiarity of it she had to admit was intriguing. And she did owe him the truth no matter how embarrassing she found it.

Chapter 5

The Steepe manor looked more foreboding this time now that she knew what awaited her. The grounds were perfectly manicured right down to the bushes beneath the windows, reminding her that the lone bush in front of the bakery could use a good trimming. A few flowers would liven the bakery up too. That would have to fall to her mother, the only one in the family with a green thumb.

The manor looked elegant despite the foreboding clouds overhead. Far too elegant for a baker's daughter. A man who lived in a home like this would marry up, not down. She couldn't understand why he'd sent her an invitation to the party in the first place. Then again, he had chosen her based on her tastes in tea. Anything could be possible with a man like that. She couldn't decide if that was exciting or terrifying.

She forced her feet forward before her nerves got the best of her. She knocked on the door, fighting the urge to turn and run. The butler answered. He was older than Mr. Steepe with the severe look of a man who didn't abide humor or dust. Or based on his reaction to Elizabeth's choice at the party, coffee. Up close, he looked nothing like Mr. Steepe. Even his hair was more of a sandy blond than Mr. Steepe's brown hair. Only a fool like her could have mistaken them.

"Excuse me, I am here to see Mr. Steepe."

"Which one, miss?"

"Which one?"

"Mr. Steepe the elder, or Mr. Steepe the younger. I'm afraid the elder is gone for business."

"Erm, Mr. Martin Steepe."

"This way." He led her to the parlor. "Whom should I say is calling?"

"His ..." She couldn't bring herself to say the word fiancée. It didn't feel right. For all she knew he could have already changed his mind on the engagement. "Miss Graham." She handed him her calling card.

"Very good." The butler left. She avoided the chaise she'd laid on during her last visit. Instead she roamed the room to admire the artwork to keep her mind busy. Old family portraits mingled with paintings of the countryside and ships. One of the ships bore a flag with the Steepe business crest.

After all this, sailing to a new country to start over sounded like a tempting plan. A change of scenery could be just the thing her imagination needed. Not that she'd leave the bakery behind. She would never hand it over to a stranger, but she wanted something of her own too. Bread never changed, but when she wrote anything felt possible. Nothing matched the pride a finished story gave her.

Before the latest string of rejections, her mind wouldn't give her a break with its constant stream of new ideas and characters. But now it was as if her imagination had shriveled up and died. Every idea she second guessed until she couldn't bring herself to write it at all.

The butler stepped back into the room, pulling her from her thoughts of blank pages. "Mr. Steepe is in his study with his cousin. Allow me to lead the way." He took her up a stately staircase. Her hand reached for the railing, and then she yanked it away. The wooden railing gleamed from a recent polishing. She didn't want to ruin the polish with fingerprints. That would be poor manners. A floral scent drifted through the air, distracting her away from the railing. Honeysuckle. The scent made her long for spring.

His study wound up being a room on the second floor that overlooked the garden out back. A small seating area sat in front of the fireplace lined by bookshelves. In front of the window sat a large desk with Mr. Steepe behind it. Or at least she assumed it was Mr. Steepe since Bertram was staring down over his shoulder. Whoever sat at the desk wore a ridiculous head contraption that held multiple magnifying glasses and hid his face. In front of him lay an umbrella with his attention focused on the handle.

"Move a bit to the right. You're blocking the sunlight," Mr. Steepe murmured. Bertram shifted.

"You don't need to fix anything. The umbrella is fine," Bertram groused.

"I wouldn't call an umbrella magicked to rain on you fine. That is the opposite of what an umbrella is meant to do."

Bertram let out an exasperated sigh. "Simply a hole in it I bet."

"No, no. It is the runes." Martin tapped on the umbrella. "You mixed this one up on the end for the symbol for dry. Currently it will rain on you whenever you open the umbrella."

Bertram's mouth twitched, his expression souring.

"All I need to do is change the last rune, and you will stay dry." They lapsed into silence while he worked and Charlotte saw her opportunity to speak.

"Hello, Mr. Steepe and Mr. Steepe."

Bertram's eyes narrowed on her.

"Miss Graham!" Martin said, his head jerking up. "How delightful to see you. Give me one moment, won't you? I'm almost done fixing Bertie's umbrella."

Bertram sniffed. "I told you I don't need help. I'm perfectly capable of doing enchantments on my own."

"Of course you are," Martin said in a voice that reminded Charlotte of the way her mother used to tell her she was good at making bread when she was a child despite all the lumps.

"Do you need anything, sir?" the butler asked. He stood in the doorway with his hands clasped behind his back.

"A tea tray please, with some sandwiches. And Lapsang Souchong tea." Martin scoured something off the umbrella handle.

"Right away, sir."

Bertram stepped around the desk and approached Charlotte. He was tall, forcing her to look up at him. Mixed with that piercing glare of his, it was hard to not feel intimidated. She squeezed her hands together to keep them from shaking. "Strange," he said.

"Your umbrella raining on you?"

His mouth twitched again. "No. I mean that it's strange I never met you before the party. With all the parties I attend, I wonder why we haven't crossed paths before? I thought I knew all the eligible young ladies of note."

Charlotte swallowed. "I'm not much of a party person."

"Well that is one thing you have in common with Marty." He leaned in closer, and she took a step back, bumping into the wall. "What was your family name again?"

She couldn't look away from his piercing brown eyes. The way he watched her made her feel like a cornered rabbit. "Umm." Her mind turned in circles, unable to concentrate. She'd already forgotten the question as she focused on his intense eyes.

"Finished!" Martin pulled the magnifying glass away from his eye and pulled the awful contraption off his head. His hair stuck out at odd angles and needed a good combing. "No more needing to worry about getting soaked by the rain." He held the umbrella out to his cousin.

Bertram yanked the umbrella away. "Thank you. You're always so willing to fix my rune mistakes, aren't you?" he said, his jaw clenching.

"Always glad to help," Martin said, seemingly oblivious to his cousin's frustration. "Are you going to stay for tea?"

"No. I have an important business meeting tomorrow I need to prepare for. We are thinking about building a sewing factory."

Martin nodded, making a noise of agreement. "I hear sewing is very profitable these days. If selling pre-cut garments made in factories for the masses works out, it would be quite the investment. Good luck."

"Indeed, although clothes are not my aim."

"Then what is?"

"Straps for rifles." Bertram turned back to Charlotte, his nostrils flaring. "You smell like cinnamon buns and bread."

She shrank under his gaze. "I do love both."

Rain pattered against the window. "Perfect timing, eh?" Martin asked. "I would have hated to see you go home soaked."

Bertram's hand clenched on his umbrella handle. "I thought the rain clouds had moved on for the day."

"Apparently not. At least it isn't snow today."

A shiny hummingbird flew in through the door, circling Bertram's head. He batted a hand at it. His hand made contact and sent the mechanical bird flying into the wall. "You still have that old thing?" He sneered.

"Of course I do," Martin said, finally sounding offended by his cousin's rude behavior. "I would never consider getting rid of it."

"I don't see why. You should have let the bird stay trash instead of fixing it." Bertram headed for the door. "Tell your mother I'll see her at the charity fundraiser later this week," Bertram called over his shoulder as he walked out.

Martin nodded but didn't respond. He moved his head contraption full of magnifying glasses to an empty spot on his shelves, setting it down with care. "Shall we sit by the fire?" he asked, his voice pleasant despite his cousin's sour attitude.

A low fire burned in the hearth. It wasn't enough to make the room hot, but it kept the damp from the rain at bay and cast a cozy glow across the room. Living above the bakery meant that space was hard to come by for her family. To have a study like this one to write in was something Charlotte could only dream of. She'd fill the shelves with penny bloods and cookbooks.

He moved to the armchair to the left of the small table, stopping to scoop up the fallen metal bird. She took the chair across from him, affording her a view of the rain. Of course she'd forgotten her umbrella. Just her luck. She'd been too worried about Mr. Steepe to remember to grab hers.

The butler entered and set the tea tray down and then retreated to hover near the door. Some sliced fruit and cheese accompanied the sandwiches.

"Beautiful day, isn't it?" Martin asked as he sat down in the opposite chair, his hair still a mess. In his hands he tinkered with the metal bird.

She looked to the window where the rain had grown harder, tapping against the window in a steady rhythm. "This morning was, yes. Did you have a good day?"

"I did," he said, his attention on the bird in his hands.

"It's a good thing you fixed your cousin's umbrella in time."

He made a noise of agreement. Not knowing what else to say she reached for her teacup. Small talk was difficult when you knew nothing about the other person. With other ladies she defaulted to discussing flower arranging, but Mr. Steepe didn't strike her as the type to have any knowledge on the best ways to arrange orchids. With nothing else to discuss, she might as well get around to the engagement. Best to get it over and done with before this grew more uncomfortable.

"I have something we need to discuss," she started. "I—"

The bird flew out of his hands, startling her. The gold and silver hummingbird moved as fast as a real one. It hovered over his head for a beat before perching on the glass jar of honey near the teapot. The bird dipped its beak into the honey. "Marvelous, isn't it?" he said when he caught her staring.

"What is it?"

"A honey dispenser." He tapped his spoon gently against his cup twice. The bird hopped over to his cup, dipping its beak in before perching back on the jar of honey. "It gives you the perfect amount for your tea. You can also whistle for the bird too, but my mother was never very fond of that." He stirred his tea and sipped at it, humming in satisfaction.

"How ... creative."

"Bertram made it for me when we were children. The bird didn't last long and so each time I fixed it I added my own additions, including the honey dispenser a few months ago. Although the early version had a few hiccups. Mainly with the bird being territorial over the honey jar. Its pecks were down right vicious."

"Are you both experienced magicians?" Despite the way she used magic at the bakery, she'd never dare call herself a magician. Her measly knowledge couldn't compare to magic like the bird or the Steepe greenhouse. It wasn't that she wasn't interested in magic. More magic had simply always been out of her reach. She didn't want to risk winding up cursed like Claude by dealing with magic she didn't understand.

Martin's expression turned serious. "My cousin has a great mind for business, but magic has never come easy to him. The hummingbird he made me when we were children fell apart within the week. Ever since I repurposed it into a honey dispenser, my mother has loved the convenience of the bird when she is taking tea in the greenhouse. I thought you might too. It's always available for your use when you visit."

Always available. The words rang in her ears. Did that mean he was expecting her to visit again? Had he not come to his senses yet? She bit her bottom lip in concentration, mimicking the way he'd tapped on his cup.

The bird hopped over to hers, dipping its long beak into her cup. After dispensing several drops of honey it flew back to perch on the jar. She stirred the honey into her tea.

"What was it you wanted to tell me?" He turned his full attention on her finally. The weight of it made her mouth go dry, and she took a long sip of her tea. What would he think when he realized he'd declared a baker's daughter his fiancée in front of everyone? It would be a scandal for him and she would be the one to blame. Oh, but the bird had put the perfect amount of honey into her tea. The realization derailed her thoughts.

"I only drink Lapsang Souchong for special occasions," she blurted out. She swallowed, all her rehearsed confessions on the way melting away as she struggled to remember them. "I find it too smoky to drink often."

"I see." He set his tea down and retreated to his desk. He rummaged through two drawers before finding what he was looking for. A small wooden ball dangled from a rope string in his hand. He sat back down and dangled the ball over her teacup. Wisps of smoke rose from her cup. The ball soaked them up. "Is that better?"

She tasted her tea. Only a hint of smokiness was left. "I didn't know magic could do such things."

He smiled. "I find magic interesting because like technology, it can make every day a little bit easier without needing to be flashy. Combined they could do amazing things together."

"I see what you mean." The magic used on their ovens helped give her family bakery an edge over their competitors. Without the magic, cooking bread and pastries at the right temperature could be tricky. Too much or too little wood on the fire would lead to burned or undercooked bread. And an uneven heat distribution would equal an uneven bake. Magic took all that guesswork out, resulting in perfectly baked goods most of the time and more bread as they spent less time worrying over the fires. "It's a shame many in the nobility don't see it the same way." Many of the old noble families actively fought against educating commoners in magic. They wanted to hoard magic to themselves as a status symbol. Technology for the commoners, magic for the rich.

"I agree. I was lucky my father could afford a tutor for me. Mixed with technology I think there is much to be achieved with magic yet." The passion in his words lit up his face, adding a becoming warmth to him. A warmth Bertram lacked.

"Magic can be far more useful than parlor tricks and entertainment. I wish more businessmen would realize how useful it can be." He pocketed the ball. "I have to be careful with this. My father left it on the desk of his study and the sun warmed it up too much. Smoke leaked out and the maids still haven't been able to get the smell out of the room. He had to replace the curtains. The rug in the room still smells like smoke on hot days." He returned to his tea, a new silence falling over them.

She popped a piece of cheese into her mouth to buy herself time to think. He didn't seem like the vengeful type, but she didn't know what type he was at all. Fixing the misunderstanding sounded simple, but sitting here made her all too aware of his higher standing and family's money. If he was the vengeful type, he could go after her family's bakery. They wouldn't be able to afford a better solicitor than whoever his money could buy. The fear clenching her stomach made it hard to swallow the cheese. She needed another gulp of tea to get the cheese down her dry throat.

A light, fast tapping on the hardwood floor made her tense. Oolong came bounding into the room, his tongue hanging out of his mouth. He ran to Martin, jumping up onto his lap and rolling onto his back for belly rubs.

"Is he your dog?" she asked, both hands squeezing her teacup. Oolong looked innocent and lovable, but so had the Hammonds' dachshunds at first. Their cute fuzziness had been disguises. They were nothing but sausages on stumpy legs filled with malice. It was as if the longer their bodies, the more destruction they wrought.

"Yes. I've loved dogs since I was five." He twisted to point at the painting above the fireplace. "That's Oolong after I first got him." A pale little boy sat curled up on a sofa with a dachshund sleeping in his lap. The boy beamed. The dog looked just like Oolong, except the painted dog had longer, darker hair than the Oolong presently on Martin's lap.

Martin pointed to a painting behind her. "And that's when I first went into business to follow in the family's footsteps." She turned. This painted dog had the right dark brown color, but he sported a white belly. Noticing her inspection as she compared them, Oolong licked the air in her direction, his head hanging upside down as Martin rubbed his stomach, and she recoiled. "Lovely."

The dog drooling on his lap couldn't be either of the painted Oolongs. This one looked like he was almost a puppy still. If Mr. Steepe was naïve enough to believe his dog had lived for almost thirty years, their engagement made a lot more sense. Then again the Hammond's dogs had proved how wicked dachshunds could be. For all she knew the beast could have entered a Faustian bargain with Satan himself.

"But no matter what changes we both always love tea. Isn't that right, Oolong?" He gave the dog's belly a vigorous rub, making his tail wagged. "His full name is Mr. Dan Cong Oolong. He's named after the phoenix oolong tea grown in China."

She gave him a strained smile. "A delightful name." But the dog was getting them off track. She straightened in her seat and brought her attention back to the problem at hand. The gentle whack, whack, whack, of Oolong's wagging tail smacking against the chair provided a steady drumbeat. "Speaking of tea, how exactly did that spell work that you used to choose me?"

He flipped Oolong over onto his stomach. "That was a bit of intricate rune work that took me several months to figure out. I designed the enchantment to pick the lady with the closest tea tastes to mine. A magical tea leaf reading of sorts. I feared the leaves might pick more than one lady, but you are the only one it chose. Right when I was worried it wouldn't pick anyone at all!" Oolong gave a low yip as if in agreement, and Martin rubbed his head.

"Now that I know you prefer lapsang for special occasions, I will be sure to have other selections on hand next time." He stood and crossed to his desk to put the ball back into his desk drawer. Oolong jumped onto the floor, sniffing at the air. He settled his front paws onto the table as he eagerly lapped up Martin's tea. Charlotte watched in horrified silence, unsure of whether she should say anything. She kept a tight hold of her cup to make sure the dog didn't get hers next. Down the hall someone whistled. The hummingbird took flight and Oolong ran after it, tongue lolling out of his mouth as his paws skidded across the hardwood floor.

Martin returned to his seat and picked up his cup, raising it to his mouth.

She pressed a hand to her mouth to hold her horror in. That same paralysis that froze her when she saw the Hammonds' dachshunds running toward her froze her now.

He finished off his tea before pouring a second cup. "Do you want me to send for a different tea?"

"No thank you," she squeaked out. She cleared her throat. "Do you think liking the same tea is enough basis for an engagement?" She sipped at her teacup to hide her nerves. The lapsang was excellent.

"Tea is one of my favorite things," he said as he leaned back, getting comfortable. "While my grandfather and father focused their efforts on the family shipping venture, my own personal business is selling tea. I wanted someone who could appreciate the business with me. It gives us at least one thing in common to start with."

She couldn't have come up with a more bizarre way of picking a bride. "And your family agreed to let you pick your fiancée in such a way?"

"My father chose my last fiancée. After that didn't end well he agreed to let me handle this one as I saw fit."

Her tea stuck in her throat and she coughed. "Excuse me, your last fiancée?" She hoped there wasn't a secret fiancée in the attic or something like the wife in Jane Eyre. She sneaked a glance at the ceiling.

His face turned grim. "My apologies. I assumed you already knew with how people gossip about my family."

Charlotte didn't know how to answer, her mind caught on the idea of there having been another before her.

"Sorry for the interruption, Mr. Steepe," the butler called from the doorway. "A gentleman from Lapsang Limited is here to see you. He says it is urgent."

Martin set his cup down. "I'm sorry, Miss Graham, but business calls and I must see to it." And then he was gone with the butler trailing after him as Martin spouted off a new tea order to him. Oolong went running past the door to follow after him.

Charlotte reached for a sandwich. By the time she finished it, no one had returned for her. She poured herself the last of the tea and polished it off. Still no one came for her. She supposed that had been goodbye then with no one to see her out. She stood to make her way toward the door, but the papers spread across the desk tempted her.

She shouldn't, she thought. Oh, but she wanted to. Who was this eccentric man who chose his fiancée by reading tea leaves? She padded on over and leaned across, being careful to not touch anything. An opened letter from Hawke House sat on the top of a small stack of unopened letters. She scanned the short letter asking Mr. Steepe if he was interested in buying the publishing house.

She sucked in a breath. If Hawke was in trouble it would explain their lack of response. Or maybe her writing had been atrocious enough that they deemed her unnecessary to reply to at all.

"Snooping, are ye?"

She jumped. Laoise cackled. "I was coming in here to dust. Didn't expect to find you." She shook the duster at Charlotte. "Naughty, naughty."

"I came over to clear up the misunderstanding about our engagement with Mr. Steepe."

"And how'd that go?"

"It hasn't, yet."

Laoise's brow wrinkled. "What?"

She threw her hands up in the air. "I didn't tell him yet who I am. The butler interrupted with something about business and he rushed off. I don't know if I'm supposed to stay here and wait for him or leave."

"If it was business you should leave or you could be waiting for hours. He's been getting ready to open some more tea shops and they have kept him busy."

"In that case you don't happen to know where Mary Hawke lives, do you? She was at the party. I'd like to call on her."

"Let's check, shall we?" Laoise whipped a sheet of paper out of her pocket, giving it a dramatic flick before unraveling it. She cleared her throat and read off Mary's address.

"Is that the guest list?" Charlotte grabbed the paper, reading the list of names and addresses. "Why do you have this?"

"A certain devastatingly handsome cousin of Mr. Steepe's was looking for it. I felt he was up to no good and so I made sure the list happened to disappear. Probably got thrown away during a cleaning, you see. If Mr. Steepe needs your address I'll volunteer to play messenger girl and hand deliver the letter."

"He may have seen me in the bakery this morning and was suspicious. I bet he is trying to figure out more about me or at the very least who I am. He was aggressive about asking why he had never met me before."

Laoise rested a hand on her hip. "He doesn't need to know anything about you. You're engaged to Martin Steepe, not his cousin."

"Only until Martin finds out who I am."

Laoise rolled her eyes. "Then don't tell him. It's as simple as that."

Charlotte lowered her voice. "You aren't suggesting I take this engagement seriously, are you? The man chose me based on tea and thinks his childhood dog is still alive."

"And he's wealthy. Marry him and you'll be set for life and living in comfort." Laoise turned to the shelves beside the desk and got to work dusting them. Most of the books were non-fiction. Books on magic, business, and finances and other boring matters dominated the shelves. Not a single penny blood in sight.

"You sound like my mother," Charlotte grumbled, glancing back at the Hawke House envelope.

"Because we are both smart. I'd take comfort over love any day."

"And that's why you aren't a romantic."

"I'm a realist," Laoise corrected. "Enough of one that if a wealthy man proposed to me I wouldn't think twice. I'd drag him to the altar the very next day." She moved on to cleaning the top of the desk, dusting around the papers instead of picking them up.

Charlotte wrung her hands. "But he is so ... odd. And not as handsome as his cousin."

"And if you married him you could spend more time writing and reading. And with his business sense you'd never need to worry about the bakery." She flicked the end of the duster at Charlotte's nose.

Put that way, Martin was a tempting prospect. Except for the whole him not knowing who she really was bit. "What happened to the previous fiancée?"

Laoise shrugged. "I don't know. I don't deal with Mr. Steepe personally much and their engagement ended right before I joined the household. They've kept mum on it."

"Maybe Mary will know something." Asking Mary might be a stretch, but who else was there to ask? If their father did business with the Steepes, surely Mary knew more about Martin than Charlotte.

"I can call a carriage around for you."

"Please do. I think I'm going to pay her a visit."

"Look at you, making new friends already." Laoise pinched Charlotte's cheek. "You'll be getting invited to all the latest parties before you know it. Ask Mary for all the gossip about Mr. Steepe.

Find out how to seduce him. I suggest learning more about tea and making friends with Oolong."

"I'm not falling into that trap. I once made the mistake of not seeing how evil cute dogs can be. I won't make the same mistake a second time."

Laoise shook her head. "You are hopeless sometimes. I'd be more than happy to take Mr. Steepe off your hands if I could."

Chapter 6

The Hawke townhouse was modest with flowers lining the walkway. Cheerful blue curtains hung in the windows. The rain poured down in buckets, making Charlotte wish she had Bertram's enchanted umbrella to help keep her dry. Preferably after Martin had fixed it. She lifted her skirts, doing her best to keep them away from all the puddles.

A harried looking maid took her to the small parlor to the right where Mary already sat near the small fire, a book in her lap. She looked up, an expression of surprise crossing her face when she spotted Charlotte.

"Charlotte! How lovely of you to visit. Please get us a pot of Earl Grey," she said to the maid. The maid left and Mary gestured to the seat beside her. "Please sit."

She inspected the room. There was no sign of any dogs, but one could never be too certain. "You don't have a dog, do you?"

Confusion tugged Mary's smile away. "Erm, no. Is that a problem?"

"I'm afraid of some dogs is all."

"My mother used to have a bird until Margaret let it fly away. Sometimes a cat visits at the back door where Margaret feeds it. But that is the only animal."

Charlotte slid into the free seat. "Thank you for accepting my visit on short notice."

Mary's smile returned. "It is my pleasure. I haven't congratulated you on your engagement yet either. I had no idea you already knew Mr. Steepe so well." She set aside her book, putting it cover side down, hiding whatever the book was.

"I didn't, but that is a long story." She couldn't shake the feeling her life was becoming nothing but her trying to explain things she also didn't understand to others. She hoped her cousin's curse wasn't rubbing off on her. "I was wondering how much you know about him? In truth I caught a glimpse of his mail and saw a letter from Hawke House. I didn't realize Mr. Steepe was connected to the company. I thought his business centered on shipping and tea."

"The parts he manages personally do, but he has investments elsewhere including with a non-fiction publisher focused on books about magic."

"Do you mean Rune Press?" She'd bought one of their books recently hoping she might find more useful spells for the bakery that couldn't curse anyone. Without hiring a magician to give them spells for outrageous sums, books were the only other option. "I ran across some of their books in my favorite bookshop. I was rather surprised to find them and rather suspicious of whether or not the magic was real. After how closely the nobles guarded their magical knowledge, I found it hard to believe someone would be willing to mass produce books about it."

Mary absent-mindedly fiddled with her charm bracelet. "They are real all right and caused quite the stir when the publisher started printing. Where the press itself is located and who works there is a closely guarded secret to keep anyone from interfering. I heard Mr. Steepe lent them books from his collection to have copied and reproduced for the masses." She stood and crossed the room to a small shelf of books. She plucked one off and handed it to Charlotte.

"A Lady's Guide to Growing and Preserving Flowers with Magic," Charlotte said, reading off the title. That explained how Mr. Steepe learned to make a magical greenhouse. On the back cover at the bottom sat the Rune Press logo. "What does the rune mean?"

"It means knowledge." Mary leaned closer with a smile. "A nobleman tried to shut the press down, but without being able to say where it was located he couldn't do anything about it. There has been a lot of speculation about Rune Press, but nothing has been proven. It seems to be its own publisher and printing press all in one."

"That is rather noble to bring more knowledge to the common people. I had no idea he was involved with Rune Press." If he was printing his own magical collection to share, she assumed his views on magic were more progressive like the other magicians without title. She sank into the armchair, the thick cushion feeling divine. With the tension of meeting Mr. Steepe off her shoulders, she found she sorely wanted a nap. She'd never known awkward engagements could be this tiring. "Does he invest in Hawke as well?"

"No, at least not yet. My father ..." Mary swallowed and pressed her hands together. "The truth is my uncle was my father's business partner until he made off with too much money to cover his gambling debts. Father has been left with the option of getting new investors or selling. He is hoping Mr. Steepe might invest in the company to keep us afloat until we can repay all our debts. Hawke was doing well up until my uncle took off."

"I'm sorry. I had no idea." There could be hope for her story yet. Charlotte had submitted INTO THE OVEN to Hawke for publication, and while she hadn't heard back, they could be ignoring it to focus on the business first. If they wound up passing after all, she'd be stuck again until she stumbled upon her next story.

"Most don't. Only those closely connected to publishing have realized Hawke is struggling."

The maid appeared with a tea tray she set down on the small table between them. Next came a full loaf of bread with some honey. The top of the bread had sunk in on itself, making it look rather pitiful.

"Sorry about the bread," Mary said once the maid left. She squirmed in embarrassment. "Father is trying to cut back on our expenses and has asked me to make all our bread instead of buying it. I don't know where I went wrong this time."

As a child Charlotte had made similar loaves. Back then her father's perfect loaves had been a marvel to her. If not for his endless patience she wouldn't have improved. "You likely let it proof too long and the dough fell in on itself when it baked."

Mary blinked at her. "Proof?"

"Proofing is when you set the dough aside to let it rise. If you let it rise too long that happens." She pointed at the bread. "Some recipes will say to let it proof for two hours, but depending on the temperature of your kitchen the dough could rise faster or need longer. The best way to ensure your dough has risen is to learn how it should look when it's ready."

"I see." Mary gave the bread a glum look. "I did get distracted by a good book when I made it. I'll set a timer next time." She cut into the bread, offering Charlotte a slice.

Charlotte accepted to be polite. "Is it that dire then that you have to make your own bread?"

Mary sighed. "Father is trying to avoid luxuries and save every coin possible to put to Hawke's debts. It's why I'm rather glad you came today. Most visitors used to be authors and booksellers, but with the company in trouble no one has been interested in visiting. Authors are looking to publish elsewhere and our editor already accepted a job with a competitor."

"That is dreadful. I'm sorry. I hope Mr. Steepe buys it if it helps." She supposed this meant she shouldn't expect a reply back to her submission. "What will happen to the authors whose stories aren't finished?" There were far too many she'd been reading the last few months that had yet to be finished. Not getting an ending to them would be maddening. It'd be like never knowing whether Dick Turpin got caught in the end for all his illicit highwayman activities. Without his former school teacher recognizing his handwriting and turning him in, she wouldn't even remember his story enough to be thinking about it right now. His downfall made his story.

"They will simply be over."

"No!" Charlotte gasped. "Even 'Twilight at Hallow Manor.'"

Mary gave another sigh. "Even 'Twilight at Hallow Manor.'" She stirred a drop of honey into her tea. Her voice went up a note. "Not that I'm invested in a dreadful story about vampires. It's just one of the most popular stories in Hawke's serials." Her thumb traced circles around a charm on her bracelet.

The floorboards creaked behind them. Margaret leaned over the back of Mary's chair. "Ugh, you aren't lamenting about your story again, are you? We both know someone else would be willing to publish you."

Mary startled, her hand knocking into her teacup. Several drops of tea sloshed out onto the tray before she caught it.

"You didn't tell me the bread was ready. Or that we had a visitor." Margaret cut herself off a thick slice and slathered it in honey. "Hi, Charlotte." She took a bite of bread. "Congratulations, by the way." The bread muffled her words.

"Margaret! Don't speak with your mouth full."

"Your story? You mean you're a writer yourself?" Charlotte asked.

"She is indeed," Margaret said. "Meet M.H. Crane, one of Hawke's leading authors." She grabbed another slice of bread before turning toward the door. Mary blushed, hissing her sister's name. "You aren't supposed to tell anyone."

Margaret shrugged. "If I were you I'd tell everyone instead of hiding behind a pen name."

Mary wiped up the spilled tea. "I have nothing to gain but unwanted attention from telling everyone."

Charlotte gaped. "You're the author of 'Twilight at Hallow Manor?' If I bring my copy of the first chapter next time will you sign it?" She had a whole pile of Hawke magazines in her room. She enjoyed rereading some of her favorites.

"Please, don't feel like you need to humor me." Mary shifted and stared down at her misshapen bread.

Charlotte put down her tea and clasped her hands together. "I just adore Lord Hallow. His brooding about his past is so mysterious. I can't wait to find out what happened that he doesn't want to talk about. And I hope the vampire hunter doesn't manage to kill him." She dropped her hands. "I have a friend who prefers the hunter, but I hope Alice ends up with Lord Hallow." It was one of the few penny bloods she'd managed to get Laoise interested in. The downside being her cheering for Lord Hallow's demise and sighing over the hunter.

Mary gave her a shy smile. "I would love to give you an autograph. Please don't tell anyone who I am. I like letting people think my pen name is a man. Makes the editors take me more seriously too, and I get to remain anonymous."

Charlotte nodded eagerly. "I won't say a word to anyone. I'm dying to find out who Alice chooses to trust."

"I've been surprised by how many readers prefer Lord Hallow. I hadn't expected that when I started writing. I thought they'd all be eager for the hunter to win. Originally in the end Alice chooses—"

"No, no. Don't spoil it!" Charlotte threw up her hands. "I don't want to know until I get there. Not knowing is what makes the story riveting." She'd gone back and forth between the vampire and the hunter at first before deciding she preferred Lord Hallow.

Mary picked at a loose thread on her sleeve. "If you are Mr. Steepe's fiancée, perhaps you could convince him to take an interest in Hawke House. Then there is no risk of 'Twilight at Hallow Manor' going unfinished."

"I could mention it to him, but I've been in his study. I didn't see a single penny blood in there. However, I'm quite certain he has every book about managing money and business ever written." She'd wished she'd taken the time for a closer look at his books on magic.

"That doesn't mean he isn't a fan of them. He could have a few tucked away in his room. I mean look at me." Mary held out her arms. "Most people don't realize I have any involvement in my father's company let alone that I'm one of their writers."

"True." But Mr. Steepe didn't strike her as the type to sneak off to read about Dick Turpin or Sweeney Todd. On the other hand she had no trouble picturing him sitting behind his desk or in his greenhouse with a book about magic or tea in his hands. "Do you by chance happen to know what happened with his last fiancée? She wasn't ... murdered ... was she?"

Mary tapped her chin with her pointer finger. "Come to think of it, no. I'm not sure what happened, just that the engagement was called off. I heard rumors she fell in love with someone else."

"That isn't hard to see why. Mr. Steepe can be rather eccentric." She couldn't think of a kinder term to use. Or a more truthful one.

"I've never met him outside of that party before, but I'm a fan of his tea. The tea shop he has is too far a walk for me to go to often enough. I'm crossing my fingers that one opens up closer to home with all the rumors flying about saying he is opening new ones." She tapped the lid of the teapot. The white porcelain had been decorated with little painted yellow and red roses winding about it. "This Earl Grey is from his shop. I swear it must be the best in all of Britain. The bergamot isn't too weak like the brand we used to get. Sometimes I suspected they didn't bother to put any in at all."

Charlotte added a dash of cream to her tea and sipped it. The balance of bergamot with the black tea leaves was perfect. She'd never tasted a better Earl Grey. "I have yet to visit the shop. I haven't been able to think about anything but Mr. Steepe."

"You should ask him to take you. It could be romantic." Mary's eyes sparkled. "And maybe you'll get free tea! That alone would be worth the visit."

"I'm not sure I should. I think Mr. Steepe might have me mixed up with someone else. It's the only way his proposal makes any sense." The truth was far too embarrassing to admit to someone she didn't know well, let alone one of her favorite writers. Enough people knew already.

Mary's face fell. "That is too bad. Perhaps my father's solicitor will manage to convince Mr. Steepe on his own."

Charlotte chewed on another bite of bread. Despite the misshapen form, the taste was almost right if not a touch too chewy. Once Mary got more practice in, she'd be able to make fine bread. "If a writer had submitted a story to Hawke House and has not heard back, can it be assumed said writer won't be hearing back?"

"Unfortunately my father isn't accepting any new writers until he gets the mess cleaned up." She refilled her teacup. "Why? Did you submit by chance?"

"Yes." Charlotte's shoulders sagged. "There had been interest, but the editor went silent on me."

"Waiting to see what happens with the company I bet." Mary stirred honey into her tea. "But if it were to be saved, you might get published." She sipped at her tea, the corners of her mouth twitching.

Charlotte took a deep breath to keep from cursing. Listening to Laoise and continuing her charade of an engagement might be worth it for a chance at publication. This would be her last chance to get her latest story serialized. Either way Mr. Steepe would be angry when he found out who she was, but why not get something out of it for herself? It was his fault anyway for proposing without clarifying her station. Why should she bear the consequences instead of him?

Outside the rain slowed to a drizzle. A plume of smoke rose into the air. "Is that a fire?"

Mary peered out the window. "Looks like it. I wonder what happened?" She jumped onto her feet. "Let's go find out. I've been trapped inside all day by the rain. Some fresh air would do me good."

"Um, all right," Charlotte said, taken by surprise by the sudden idea. As the guest, she felt it only polite to follow Mary's wishes. She hurried to gulp down her tea.

"We're stepping out, we'll be right back!" Mary called up the stairs. She got a thump in response. Mary rushed for her shoes and coat, Charlotte hurrying to keep up with her enthusiasm. Charlotte helped herself to one of the umbrellas by the door.

"I don't know if this is a good idea," Charlotte said as she chased after Mary who stepped outside with gusto, her long strides difficult to keep up with.

"It is better than sitting inside and watching it rain while worrying over my father's company. It looks like the smoke is coming from the warehouses." She pointed toward the smoke. "The closest ones aren't far from here."

"Going into the warehouse district sounds dangerous." She'd read about plenty of muggings, murders, and brawls that happened near the warehouses in penny bloods and the newspapers.

"Doesn't it?" Mary said, the sparkle back in her eye.

Oh no, Charlotte thought. Mary was one of those writers. The kind who wasn't content to simply read and enjoy danger safely from the comfort of one's own chair. They wanted to experience it too. Charlotte would rather be safely tucked away and warm in front of the fireplace than trudging through the drizzling rain toward who knew how many thieves and rough men. Thinking about it made tingles of excitement go down her neck. It felt as thrilling as the stories that kept her awake at night afraid the tapping outside wasn't from the street cat but a vampire come to claim her blood. She opened her umbrella, using it to cover both of them.

"Good thinking grabbing that. We could always use it to fight a mugger off."

If someone mugged them, Charlotte wouldn't hesitate to jab him in his sensitive bits. That'd teach any mugger to mess with a lady with an umbrella.

The smoke grew thicker as they approached, both of them huffing to catch their breath. The acrid scent burned Charlotte's nose and stung her eyes. The rain left the air damp, the soot of the city clinging to her clothing and skin. Carriages and wagons clattered by, forcing them to dodge the splashing from the wheels. Townhouses gave way to businesses and then warehouses. A tall man rushed past them, bumping into Charlotte's arm in his haste. His suit looked far too fine for the area compared to the dirty workers heading toward the smoke. She turned to admonish him, but he was already jogging around the corner.

"That man looked like Mr. Steepe's cousin."

"Did he? I didn't notice." Mary looked all about, her eyes bright and refusing to linger anywhere for more than a moment. "I'd be more worried about the man standing over there watching us." Charlotte followed her gaze. A man standing against a building lifted his newspaper, hiding his face. Around them men rushed toward the fire shouting for the fire brigade. Mary clutched at Charlotte's arm. "The fire brigade! I hope we get to see them at work."

"I've never watched them before." She squeezed Mary's arm back, watching in fascination as the brigade pulled up. Charlotte counted ten men who gathered around the fire engine on wheels to pump water from the water main while the smoke grew thicker. Her eyes watered, but the thrill of watching kept her glued in place. Warehouse workers gathered around to gawk.

"What happened?" a voice boomed out. Bertram. He stepped down from his carriage. Amongst the soot covered workers in rough clothes, soot already sticking to his stylish suit.

"A small fire, sir," one of the firemen called out.

Bertram scoffed. "Clearly. I want to know why there is a fire in my warehouse."

Finally water gushed from the hose as both women gasped in excitement. The fireman turned his attention from Bertram to the pump.

"He really is handsome isn't he?" Mary asked, her gaze drifting to Bertram.

"Handsome but rude." Too rude to make his handsome features worth looking at, she decided.

Bertram checked his pocket watch. "How much is this going to cost?" He asked when he returned his attention to the warehouse.

"What do you think caused the fire?" Mary whispered. "A brawl?"

"Someone trying to cover up a murder?" Charlotte guessed. The narrow and dim alleyway between warehouses was the perfect setting for dirty deeds.

"Or arson from a business competitor. I hear businessmen can be cutthroat."

"Do you think Mr. Steepe has enemies?"

"Who wouldn't when you have the Steepes' influence?" Mary rubbed her hands together. "It must have been quite the rivalry for someone to attempt this."

The idea unsettled Charlotte. As eccentric as Mr. Steepe was, he'd been far kinder to her than his cousin.

They watched as the firemen finished dousing the flames. It didn't take long. Foremen chased workers back to work. The watching crowd took off like marbles bumping into each other.

"Consider yourself lucky for the rain," the fireman told Bertram. "The dampness helped suppress the small fire. It'd take a larger fire to burn it all down in this weather." A hushed talk ensued with much hand waving from Bertram and frowning from the fireman.

Charlotte approached Bertram, her and Mary both staying huddled under the umbrella. If she was going to pretend to be engaged to his cousin a little longer, offering a hand would be the right thing to do.

"Is there anything I can do to help, Mr. Steepe?"

He turned to her, his confusion turning to a sour look when he recognized her. "Miss Graham," he said, his voice dry. His gaze lingered on Mary. "And Miss …" An awkward silence descended on them.

"Hawke," Mary supplied.

"I suggest you both go back to wherever you came from. There is nothing you can do here."

A second carriage pulled up behind Bertram's. Martin stepped out, a large umbrella in hand. The rain didn't touch the umbrella, instead bouncing away from whatever enchantment he had on it. He took in the fire brigade and the light smoke still drifting into the sky. "I heard there was a fire."

Bertram's look of annoyance faded to one of pity as he rested a hand on his cousin's shoulder. "Half of our stored goods are burnt to a crisp and the rest are smoke damaged. I'm afraid your teas are ruined. I'm very sorry."

Martin's mouth puckered as he registered the news, his gaze flickering over the warehouse. Then he mimicked Bertram's pose, clapping Bertram's shoulder. "No, no, I must extend my condolences to you. I cleared out all my teas last week and moved them to my shops. I wasn't planning on having anything else in there until my next shipment."

Bertram's face reddened, his hand clamping down on Martin's shoulder. His eyes bulged.

"There, there." Martin pulled his cousin into a hug. Bertram's arms flailed as Martin patted his back. "I will help you recoup your losses. This will be nothing but a small bump in the road."

Bertram pulled away, straightening his coat and attempting to dust the soot off his sleeve, which resulted in him smearing it. He gave up with a huff. "I don't need any pity."

"Do you know how the fire started?" Charlotte asked.

Martin blinked at her in surprise. Then he smiled. "Miss Graham, how wonderful to see you," he said as if they had stumbled upon each other in Hyde Park instead of in the drizzling rain beside his smoking warehouse.

"Not yet," Bertram answered.

"Did anyone see a suspicious character about by chance?" Mary asked. She lowered her voice and rubbed her hands together again. "Maybe a man in a long coat or with a strange scar on his face?"

"What?" Bertram asked, his forehead creasing in confusion.

"I think I saw Mr. Steepe running from the warehouse on our way here," Charlotte said. Seeing his unforgettable jaw up close made her sure of it.

When everyone gave her a look of confusion, she pointed at Bertram. "That Mr. Steepe."

He stuck his nose in the air. "Preposterous. As you can see I came by carriage from my business meeting at my future factory location."

"Bertram wouldn't burn his own stock," Martin said, as if it were a ludicrous notion. "That would be silly and make no financial sense at all."

"Exactly." Bertram said, straightening his coat again. "Now if you'll excuse me, I'm going to go see the damage inside for myself." He marched off, his shoulders stiff.

Martin remained, a placid smile on his face. He didn't speak, offering no conversation. The drizzling rain grew heavier.

Mary looked to Charlotte for guidance. Finally Charlotte cleared her throat. "Mr. Steepe, would you be kind enough to escort us back to Mary's house? The weather is dreadful for walking today."

He nodded. "Certainly, Miss Graham. I will take you in my carriage." He rushed ahead of them to open the carriage door.

"He's awkward, but sweet," Mary whispered.

"I think you are underestimating that first one."

"Better than awkward and not sweet."

"True enough." Charlotte let Mary climb in first while she held the umbrella.

"Miss Graham," Martin said when she stepped up to the door. "By chance are you free Friday afternoon? I would like to host you in my garden for tea."

The offer surprised her enough she couldn't find an answer right away. Here his warehouse was smoldering and he was thinking about tea this Friday.

His face fell. "I understand if you are busy. I can show you some of my other teas another time."

"No, Friday is fine. I'd love to come have tea with you. Are you sure you will be available with this warehouse situation?"

"Don't trouble yourself about the warehouse. We have excellent insurance. I'd rather let them handle it while I take tea with you." He smiled at her and a single butterfly took flight in her stomach.

"Me too," she murmured.

Chapter 7

O n Friday, Mr. Steepe greeted her at the door and proffered his arm to lead her to the garden. Laoise pretended to dust the banister as she watched them go by, the duster whacking against the spindles as her aim fell off.

This time a single table for two sat in the center of the garden near the fountain. The bubbling water of the fountain soothed her nerves. The sun peeked out from the gray clouds. A tray piled high with light snacks sat in the center of the table. A tea cart sat off to the side and a maid stood at a respectable distance, but close enough to be ready to give assistance.

"You have a beautiful garden." She would love to see it in full bloom someday. To sit under a tree for shade and write.

"The flowers are my mother's pride. My father's business keeps him away more often than not, and so she spends her time out here as her work." He held out her chair for her. "I loved the garden as a child. When I was too sick to run and play I could at least sit out here with a book when mother let me visit the city. But these can't compare to the gardens at our countryside retreat."

She thought back to the family portrait in the parlor. How wane he'd looked in it. "Were you sick often?"

"For several years, yes. I spent most of it in the family home out in the countryside. The doctor said the fresh air would be good for me." His expression grew troubled. "In fact there was a year when my parents feared I wouldn't make it to see Christmas. My mother commissioned a family portrait afraid there wouldn't be another one, and my father began training Bertram to be his heir instead." He sat down across from her. "But as you can see, here I am and as healthy as a horse thanks to my doctor."

"That must have been very hard for you." And yet he'd been smiling in the portrait. She admired that. If she ever faced such a trial she hoped she could greet it with the same good cheer. If only she could say the same about the current state of her writing. Or rather, the lack thereof.

"It was, but it gave me plenty of time to read and practice magic. Oolong was at my side through it all, and Bertram visited me often. My mother insisted on tending to me herself. She always made my tea." He reached for the tea set and placed a small blue cup in front of her. "Because of her, a hot cup of tea always feels like a warm hug to me."

She laid a hand over her heart as his words settled in there. "That is very sweet. I never considered tea in those terms before, but it is true." She inspected the cart. At least a dozen tins sat crowded on it. "Is it safe to assume these are all your teas?"

He smiled and cast a look of pride at the tins. "Yes. I wasn't sure what you might like, so I brought some of my other favorites and bestsellers. What kind of tea do you like? Black tea? Herbal tea? Fruity flavors?" He leaned forward, giving off the air of an eager puppy.

"We never keep anything exotic on hand. We tend to drink Earl Grey, English Breakfast, and my mother has an apple herbal that is quite good." Her mornings were busy enough she barely had time to notice the taste of her tea. Thanks to the new assistant, she might not need to rush straight out of bed and to the kitchen anymore. She'd have plenty of time to enjoy a morning cup. "Of course I'd love to try something new if you have any recommendations for me."

He hummed and hawed as he examined the cart's offerings. She turned to get a better view of all the overwhelming options. Without him to help her choose she wouldn't know where to start.

"Would you be interested in a hazelnut black? It is very popular with the ladies who frequent my shop. With a little cream added it makes for a great dessert tea."

"Yes, please. A hazelnut tea sounds delicious." Her mouth watered.

He prepared the teapot and then reached for the kettle, inspecting it. He set it back down. "My apologies. It seems the water has cooled too much. I'll send for fresh hot water."

"No need. We can use magic to heat the water up, right?" Just like the oven at the bakery. As long as the water was still warm the same runes should do the trick.

Embarrassment crossed his features, making him shift in his seat. "I'm afraid I don't know any runes for that off the top of my head. I would have to consult my books."

"I can do it." She held out her hands for the kettle.

He gave her a skeptical look but handed it over.

She picked up her spoon, using the handle like a quill to avoid burning herself on the hot metal of the kettle. She pressed the spoon and thought of the runes. The amount of time she'd traced over them on the oven should have burned them into her memory, but without the carving as a guide she found herself unsure.

She started out slowly, her movements growing faster as her confidence grew. After the first rune the rest were easy, a simple matter of muscle memory. He jumped up to watch over her shoulder, his breath tickling her ear. That bergamot smell of his wafting over her nose. Her pulse picked up and she couldn't tell if it was because she was nervous or excited by the closeness. Perhaps a bit of both.

She finished, but the weak light from the runes faded away without the flare that signaled the spell had been activated. She wrinkled her nose at it. "Maybe it only works on ovens. I've never used the magic on anything else before."

"I think you turned this rune sideways. Fixing it should do the trick." He reached over to the kettle, his hand brushing against the back of hers and sending goosebumps shooting up her arm. Her thoughts scattered. He retraced the runes, turning the first one ninety degrees. The runes flashed and steam erupted from the pot. She jumped in surprise.

"Marvelous! I've never seen a Latin spell mixed with Gaulish runes like that."

"Gaulish? I'm not familiar." It sounded like some kind of fish.

"It's an ancient Celtic language. I learned about it when I spent a summer in France."

"I didn't know the runes were ... Gaulish. The rune spell has been passed down through my family." She couldn't think of any way to pretend she was as traveled as he was. She'd never been to France, let alone spent a summer there. It was one of many reminders that she stood far below him.

"Does that mean you don't have a book about these runes?"

"No. I have no idea where my grandfather learned them. I understand it was hard for anyone who wasn't wealthy to get a hold of rune spells back then."

"It was," he murmured as he moved back to his seat, feet shuffling in disappointment. Her shoulder felt cold without his warmth. She bit her bottom lip as her mind searched for an idea to call him back. Too soon he was already back in his seat.

He poured the water into the teapot and turned over the hourglass. "And a shame too. I would have loved to have studied the book that spell came from. There are quite a few books on magic that I've found difficult to find copies of. Even public libraries tend to only have the most rudimentary guides."

"Are you searching for books for your printing press?" She needed to remember to thank Mary later for that tidbit.

"And personal use. I try to read every book before passing it onto my printer." He closed the tin of tea and returned it to the cart. "I didn't know you knew about my printing press. Most people don't know I'm the one who runs it."

"I have a friend with ties to publishing, Mary Hawke, who told me. I have one of your press's books at home, but I haven't found the time to read it yet."

He sat up straighter. "Which one?"

"Practical Uses for Magic in the Home." What she'd taken a peek at hadn't been very practical in her opinion. Too much glamor for making one's complexion more milky or eyes brighter. A lot of the magic could be achieved with cosmetics instead. There was a section on entertaining guests, but she thought servants would be the more practical option in that regard. Although to be fair to the book she had wanted to read more about the runes to keep smoke from the fireplace out of the house. That spell looked as practical as the title advertised.

"I'm familiar. That one is very popular with noble ladies I understand. My mother has a copy that was passed down through her family after her grandmother married the third son of a baron."

"My family doesn't have many family heirlooms like that, but your press seems to be quite the feat according to my friend. You haven't read any books by Hawke House, have you? They do a lot of serials."

His brow creased. "I'm afraid I'm not familiar with their work. I will have to look into them."

The hourglass ran out and the teapot rose into the air as if held by invisible hands. She jerked her hand away from her cup as the teapot poured itself, filling her cup before moving on to Mr. Steepe's who didn't blink an eye at it. "An enchanted teapot?"

He beamed. "Yes. The enchantment ensures the tea gets poured right on time instead of getting over steeped. The hourglass isn't even needed." He tapped the hourglass. "I've been using it to ensure the enchantment works properly. I'm hoping to sell enchanted teaware like this in my shop soon."

Magic for tea! She'd never heard of such a thing before. "Would you let me know when you do? A teapot like this would delight my mother. She has a habit of letting it brew a bit too long." During the morning rush it always ended up over steeped, turning the flavors bitter.

He nodded. "Mine too. She can never remember how long to steep each kind. In fact that is what inspired me to apply magic to teapots. Giving my mother perfectly brewed tea without any fuss was well worth the research. She made me excellent tea for many years, and I can finally repay the favor."

She smiled. His clear love for his mother was adorable, and she understood it. If she could find any magic to help the bakery she would use it in a heartbeat. A rune spell to give bread the perfect rise would save them a lot of grief. If she had access to all his books on magic, how else might she be able to apply it to the bakery?

She sipped at her cup and he watched her.

"Do you like it?"

The drink was smooth and the hazelnut flavoring just right without overpowering the tea leaves. She took another sip, closing her eyes and tipping her head back as she savored the flavors. "Mmm, delicious."

He smiled, looking pleased with himself. "It is one of my own blends."

"You don't happen to have a chamomile on that cart, do you? My mother used to give it to me before bed when I was growing up." Come to think of it, her mother quit buying chamomile when she switched to her new herbal tea. Charlotte missed it. Chamomile had helped her sleep at night. She always fell asleep easier when she drank it.

"Certainly. I would be happy to brew it next for you to try. Chamomile is great for relaxation. I often serve it at business meetings."

She took another long sip of her tea, enjoying the flavor and the way the tea warmed her. Afternoon tea was turning out to be far more pleasant than she'd expected. She could almost forget about a fiancée hidden somewhere in his attic and how furious he might be when he found out she was a baker's daughter. If only she could have a real courtship spent sipping away in the garden discussing magic.

"There you are!" Bertram's voice rang out over the garden. He carried a small box in his hands. "I brought you a treat to go with your tea." He grabbed the chair from a table tucked into a corner of the garden on his way over to them. He joined them, Charlotte eyeing him with skepticism. After the warehouse fire, she didn't trust him. She was certain it'd been him she saw. Why he'd been running from the fire she couldn't say, and that was precisely what left her feeling unsettled by the experience.

"Would you like some tea?" Martin asked. He lifted the teapot. "I can make a new pot."

"I can warm up the water for you with magic," Charlotte added.

Bertram wrinkled his nose. "Please tell me you aren't making a beautiful flower like your fiancée get hot water for you. Ladies should not need to sully their hands with magic or such mundane tasks."

"I'm not a delicate flower," Charlotte mumbled. She'd accept the beautiful part though. She wasn't one to turn down a compliment like that no matter who it came from.

Bertram ignored her. "I came to bring you these." Bertram opened the box, presenting them with several cinnamon buns inside. "Do you know what bakery these are from?" He asked, keeping his eyes locked onto Charlotte's.

Charlotte's heart skipped a beat. He knew. No wonder he didn't like her.

"My favorite bakery!" Mr. Steepe declared. "Thank you, Bertie. How considerate of you."

Bertram scowled. "Bertram," he corrected. "Bertie is a childish name."

"I think it suits you."

Bertram shook the box of cinnamon buns in Charlotte's direction. "Would you like to try one? You might recognize the bakery."

"I would love one." Martin reached over and grabbed the closest bun.

"I think I'll save mine for later." She didn't need to look long at the cinnamon buns to recognize them as the ones she made that morning. With the new assistant and her cousin, her father no longer needed her in the kitchen every day, but she didn't know what else to do with herself.

Bertram's smile cracked. He finally turned to Martin. "You should know on my way over here I saw your honey hummingbird get out of the house again. Oolong was chasing it."

Mr. Steepe's eyes widened in alarm. "Where?" He stood up. Knocking his chair over in his haste.

"Near the front door."

"I hope he doesn't try eating the bird again. He choked on it last time." He jogged off, calling for Oolong.

As soon as Mr. Steepe was out of ear shot, Bertram leaned toward Charlotte. "I know who you are, and I'm not letting a commoner marry my cousin." He reached into his pocket and slammed something onto the table. He let go and the broken hummingbird's silver wings twitched. "I'm going to be generous and give you a chance to tell him yourself."

Her mouth went dry. The bird's wings twitched at the same time as her heart. She'd known the courtship couldn't last, but she'd expected more time to press Hawke's case. More time to get to know Martin and drink his fabulous tea. She wasn't ready for it all to be over yet. "Who he marries isn't your decision."

Bertram rolled his eyes. "Martin should be aiming for a title. His parents won't let him marry you, and I don't care how you tricked him into proposing." He leaned back, satisfied with himself. He whistled, the hummingbird's wings twitched in response. "Over here, Martin!" He lowered his voice. "Confession time."

"I didn't trick him." She glared at him, her hands twisting together on her lap.

Martin reappeared, a wiggling Oolong under one arm.

"Your hummingbird is broken. You'll have to retire it I'm afraid."

"Nonsense," Martin said. "New wings and it will work again." He set Oolong down and the dog took off after a small butterfly that stayed within the warmth of the greenhouse.

Bertram tapped Charlotte's foot with his. "Miss Graham has something she needs to tell you."

The sun disappeared behind a cloud and she shivered. Without the sun the air felt as cold as Bertram's predatory smirk.

Martin gave her a look of concern. "Is something amiss?"

"I ..." Imagining the way he might react stole her voice away. Thinking of him getting mad at her made her stomach twist.

Martin's forehead wrinkled as his concern deepened. The worry in his eyes felt kind to her and it made her want to hold on a little longer to that kindness and to whatever other magical surprises he still held. Behind Martin the butterfly landed on Oolong's nose and the dog froze.

"Go on," Bertram encouraged as he plucked a scone off the tray. "Best to get dreadful business out of the way."

"I'm afraid of dogs," she blurted out. Bertram's expression turned stormy and as he opened his mouth to object, she blazed on, refusing to let him. "I don't want to be afraid, it's just that there was an incident with the Hammonds' dachshund. Or two. Maybe three. In truth I don't remember how many dogs were involved, but I haven't been able to bring myself to pet one since."

Martin lifted a hand to his chest, mouth falling open. "Oh my, that is dreadful."

"I could have sworn you meant to tell him something else," Bertram said, pinning her under his expectant gaze.

She looked away from him. "I was afraid to tell you because of Oolong. I know he is precious to you."

Martin rallied, throwing his shoulders back. "Don't you worry. Oolong would never hurt you. I can put him back inside if he makes you nervous. I'm sure with time you'll warm up to him."

"Perhaps we should all go inside," she said as she rubbed her arms. "It is starting to get rather chilly out here with the sun hidden." There was no fire today. Leaving them to rely on the sun.

"No, no," Bertram said as he reached for a napkin. "No reason to cut this tea of yours short. It's too perfect a time to get everything out in the open. I'll take care of the cloud for you."

"And I'll make you some chamomile tea to warm you up," Martin said as he grabbed the tin behind him.

Bertram wrote a long string of runes onto the napkin. Martin stuck a finger in the air. "Bert—"

"Not now," Bertram snapped as he continued writing.

Martin fisted a hand and pressed it against his mouth as he watched, hiding his grimace. Then Bertram tossed the napkin into the air with a few words that sounded like gibberish to Charlotte. The napkin floated up and then disintegrated.

"There. You'll have sunshine back in but a moment. Please continue telling Martin about everything you've been meaning to tell him." He crossed his arms and leaned back.

Martin watched the sky. "I don't think that's going to happen. I meant to tell you that you wrote the runes in the wrong order."

"I did what?" Bertram glanced up too. Charlotte followed suit. The cloud in front of the sun didn't seem to move at all, until she realized it was growing. No, that wasn't quite right. The cloud descended on them, casting a thick, wet fog over the garden, covering everything outside of the greenhouse in a thick layer of dew.

Bertram squeezed the arm of his chair, nostrils flaring. Charlotte hugged herself, shivering at the sudden drop in temperature.

"Don't be hard on yourself," Martin said as he patted his cousin's arm. "Weather magic is tricky and doesn't work most of the time even when done right. I suppose that's why there's still poor weather to worry about!"

Somewhere in the fog Oolong whined, stopping when Martin called for him. The dog ran head first into Charlotte's legs. He cocked his head as he locked up at her. She froze, wondering if the dog could sense her nerves. Martin called him again and Oolong changed course to plop down at Martin's feet.

Martin gave Charlotte a strained smile. "Shall we move this indoors?"

"Please do." If they stayed out much longer she would catch a cold with how her dress soaked up the damp air.

He offered her his arm as Bertram trudged down the garden path. Oolong ran after him, tripping Bertram. Bertram stumbled and caught himself against a tree. Oolong didn't break stride as he ran ahead. Bertram grumbled under his breath.

"I'm sorry about the weather," Martin said, voice apologetic. "I was hoping to have a lot more time with you in the garden."

"It isn't your fault. Getting to try your tea was lovely."

"I'm glad you enjoyed it. I'll find more teas you enjoy next time."

Oolong met them at the stairs and the butler met them at the door, holding it open for them. "Miss Graham. Mr. Steepe. Mr. Oolong," he greeted as they walked in. "Shall you be needing new tea, Mr. Steepe?"

"Yes. Please have everything brought to the parlor."

"Heavens! What happened to the weather?" Martin's mother asked. She sat in the window seat with a book on her lap, chewing on her bottom lip as she watched the fog.

"It won't last more than an hour or two," Martin said.

Bertram gave her a strained smile. "Good afternoon, Auntie."

"Bertie! Always a delight to have you visit." Martin's mother hopped up from her seat. "I'm glad you are all here. I was hoping to extend a dinner invitation for Sunday to everyone and since I seem to have lost Miss Graham's address ..." She gave them a nervous smile.

Bertram's sour look changed in an instant, his charming smile reappearing. "I would love to Auntie, as always." He turned to Charlotte. "You will join us, won't you, Miss Graham? We would love a chance to get to know my dear cousin's fiancée better." He wrapped an arm around Martin's shoulders. All eyes turned to Charlotte.

Charlotte swallowed. "I would love to come."

Bertram's smile turned wolfish. "Excellent. I'm sure we will all be looking forward to it."

"Indeed," Charlotte said, wishing she could throw all the cinnamon buns he'd brought at his face.

A knock on the door startled them all. The butler dropped the tea cart off in the hallway and swept past them. At the door a burly man in sooty clothes tipped his hat to the butler. The hat looked too small for him, sitting higher than it should. The man looked like he belonged at the docks instead of on the Steepe's doorstep. "Package for Mr. Bertram Steepe." A small crate rested in the man's hands.

"He's here." The butler stepped aside and waved at the man to bring the package in. The cracked lid let an acrid smell escape. Charlotte covered her nose.

"What is that scent?" Charlotte coughed.

Bertram rushed to the crate, beginning his sentence twice as he tripped over his words before making sense. "Wrong house! Outside with it!" He stood in front of the crate, hiding it from view as he backed out of the house.

"Don't forget about Sunday dinner!" Martin's mother called after him as he shuffled out behind the crate.

The butler closed the door behind him. "Tea is ready," he announced as he steered the cart to the small table by the windows.

"Excellent." Martin pulled out a chair, gesturing for Charlotte to sit.

The two of them settled in at the table, his mother moving elsewhere in the house. From her perch beside the window, she watched Betram gesture wildly at the man and his crate. The man started to set the crate down and Bertram jabbed at his chest, using his other hand to point at his carriage.

"That was odd, wasn't it?" Charlotte asked as she watched Bertram climb into his carriage.

Martin shrugged. "We emptied out the warehouse for repairs. He has to find somewhere to store what survived. I wish I had space at my tea shops to offer him storage, but I'm all full." His fingers rested on one of his tea tins. "How about chamomile this time?"

"Sounds perfect," she said, still distracted by Bertram's carriage as it pulled away. He knew who she was. How long did that give her to confess first?

Chapter 8

"Bertram is going to tell everyone the truth at the family dinner, I know it," Charlotte lamented. The bakery's kitchen was empty except for her and Laoise. Her cousin would be back soon to start proofing more dough and the assistants would arrive before dawn. But for a brief hour they had the kitchen to themselves.

Laoise chewed on her slice of brioche. Charlotte had already eaten enough bread to make her stomach ache, but it did nothing to calm her emotions.

"Well he hasn't tattled on you yet. I'd have heard by now if he had."

"He's probably just waiting to humiliate me in front of Martin."

"Maybe he already told him and he didn't care. Or he told him and he forgot. Your Mr. Steepe isn't exactly..." she trailed off, stuffing her face. Charlotte held a little hope for the former, but had far more confidence in the latter theory. "I thought you didn't want to court him anyway?"

"I didn't think I did. Or rather I didn't think I truly had a chance. A man like him with a baker's daughter? I hate that I've learned enough about him to start liking him. To want to know more about him." She wondered if she should knead dough instead of eating bread. Pretending the dough was Bertram's face might feel good. "But he was nice and the garden was relaxing. He likes magic and wouldn't it be fun to learn more? And his tea was some of the best I've ever had." She sighed as she slouched against the table. "His rejection is going to hurt."

"Wow, good tea and nice? What high expectations," Laoise said through a mouthful of brioche. "But I can understand the magic. Although it's a little unnerving when his hummingbird goes whizzing past my head in the kitchen. Sometimes it makes the cook scream." Laoise snorted at the memory.

"Once Bertram tells everyone who I am, the courtship will be over." Despite the stomach ache she considered taking another slice of bread. "I wasn't worried about marrying. I always figured I would work at the bakery whether any courtships panned out or not, but now that sounds lonely. I'm getting tired of staring at the same kitchen day in and out."

Laoise finished off her bread. "Then don't let that devil with an angel's face win. Fight back. I'm sure he has something you could blackmail him with. He is a businessman." She poked at the empty plate. "Got any more brioche?"

"I saved you this." Charlotte whipped the kitchen towel off the basket beside her, revealing the pastie beneath.

Laoise snapped it up and bit into it, her eyes closing in delight. "Remember that odd package that came today? I heard Bertram tell the man it should have gone to the docks. Odd, don't you think?"

"Yes. He almost seemed scared that it'd come to the Steepe manor." Of all the suspicions she harbored about him, this one ranked the highest. And yet like all the other suspicions she could go on nothing but her hunch.

"If you like Mr. Steepe, fight back. Beat his cousin at his own game and win your fair prince's heart once and for all." Her gaze wandered to the doorway. "And speaking of princes, is your father home?"

Charlotte rolled her eyes. "No, he's already in bed."

Laoise dropped her chin into her hands. "How disappointing."

She pushed her tea aside. It reminded her too much of her time with Martin. "I'm starting to think you come to see him instead of me."

"Of course I come to see you, but your Da is a nice bonus." She sighed. "A nice, muscular bonus."

Charlotte tossed the towel at her.

Laoise batted it aside. "As far as your problem goes, I will forever stand by Mr. Steepe being a good enough choice. Why shouldn't girls like us get our chance to marry men like him? With all the work I do I should be named a countess." Laoise laughed. "Wouldn't that be something?"

"You'd be the best countess around."

"And I'd hire your father to be my personal baker."

Charlotte groaned. "You need to get over him."

"Maybe someday." Laoise's eyes went distant.

Charlotte snapped her fingers in front of Laoise's face to get her attention back. "Bertram said his cousin should aim for title."

"But is that what Mr. Steepe cares about?"

"I ... don't know. I didn't ask."

Laoise finished off her pastie. "Then let's take that as you still have a chance. Go snoop around and find something to use against Bertram. He deserves to be tormented." Her mouth puckered.

"You really don't like him, do you?"

She shoved the empty plate away with more force than necessary. "He has a habit of spilling his tea and guess who gets to clean up his messes?" She pointed both thumbs at herself. "And he calls me Louise instead of Laoise in that posh accent of his that makes me want to put my foot up his behind every time. The least you could do for me is marry his cousin and torment him with the knowledge every day." She smiled, resting her chin on her hand. "I would love to watch him squirm at the wedding. I would pay to see that."

"Do you want to come snooping with me? See what we can find?" She'd missed their time together. Ever since Laoise started working as a maid and her brother's sickness returned, it was rare for them to get time alone together.

Laoise's good humor disappeared. She stared down at her tea. "I can't. I promised to drop off some candy for John tonight and visit him tomorrow. Mum says he is on the verge of another bout of illness."

That statement was akin to a cold bucket of water being thrown on Charlotte. "I'm so sorry. Next time I'll save a treat for him." Laoise's younger brother was only seven. The health struggles started with a cough when he was a babe and refused to let go. They'd gotten worse over the past year with no signs of letting up. Charlotte squeezed Laoise's hand.

Laoise squeezed back. "Mum appreciates the bread your send over every week."

"Let us know if you need anything else."

"We will." A wicked smile crossed her face. "You can kiss Mr. Steepe and tell me how it goes."

Charlotte groaned again. "You know that's not what I meant."

Laoise replied by puckering her lips and making kisses at her. "Oh, Mr. Steepe," she said in a poor imitation of Charlotte, "kiss me again."

"I do not sound like that! Go see your brother. And forget about me kissing anyone."

Laoise made more kissy noises as she left, cackling as she went out the door. With Laoise unable to go snooping with her, she'd have to find someone else.

Mary's bread was better this time with no dent in the middle. By the looks of it, she'd gotten the proofing right.

"Your advice worked," Mary declared as she offered Charlotte a slice. The inside of the bread proved to be fluffier this time instead of dense. Charlotte nibbled on it while she explained why she wanted Mary to visit the docks with her. With Laoise unable to join her, Mary had been the only other person she could think of. As nervous as she had been about asking, Mary didn't once stop to ask any questions. She nodded, encouraging Charlotte.

"A stakeout! How fun!" Mary said once Charlotte finished explaining. "I'll get the costumes."

"Costumes?" Charlotte couldn't figure out where or how the conversation had gotten away from her already. Mary's enthusiasm for excitement had a way of pulling her forward faster than anticipated.

"Can I come?" Margaret called down the stairs. "Safety in numbers, remember?"

"That is true," Mary murmured. Then her mouth twisted as she registered the questions. "Margaret! We've discussed your eavesdropping habit just yesterday." She turned toward the stairs, hands on her hips, just as Margaret peeked into the doorway.

"It's not eavesdropping when I'm not trying to listen in. Everything echoes up the stairs. So, can I come? Going to the docks sounds like fun."

"That isn't my decision to make." They both looked to Charlotte.

Charlotte stammered, unsure of what was happening. "Any help I can get," she settled on.

"Then we should leave right away. Don't want to get caught out too late." Mary rubbed her chin while she mumbled over costume ideas.

Next thing Charlotte knew, Mary was pulling her up the stairs to change them both into men's clothing. Once Mary was satisfied with Charlotte's outfit, she got to work on her own costume while Charlotte stared at all the outfit options. There was a maid uniform, plenty of men's clothing, and quite a few hats. Charlotte felt as impressed as she did unnerved. "Do you do this often?"

"Often enough," Mary said as she flipped through the shirts. "I like melting into the background to observe where no one will recognize me. It lets me see and experience things I couldn't as Mary Hawke without being stopped by anyone who might recognize me. It makes for good writing material. Plus, we could never walk down to the docks as ourselves. We'd draw too much attention."

"I've never considered dressing up before. I write about bakeries because it is what I know and feel confident writing about."

"Did the story you submit to Hawke include a bakery?" Mary settled on a costume and changed.

Charlotte heaved a sigh. "Yes, and I'm coming to terms with the fact that I can't compete with The String of Pearls. I'm trying to figure out my next book, but it has been harder than usual. I used to have more ideas than time to write, but they have all dried up and I can't figure out how to make any of them work."

"Writer's block," Mary said as she pulled a man's shirt on.

Charlotte cringed at hearing the dreaded phrase. She loathed the term. It made her imagine a wall of bricks blocking off her imagination. "I've stuck to writing what I know." She'd already nixed the idea of writing about a struggling writer several times. Too cliché.

Mary pulled on a plain necklace with a rune engraving on the copper square and hid it beneath her coat. "I see a lot of writers take that advice literally, but that is what imagination and empathy is for. I don't write about vampires because I am or want to be one, but because I like to imagine what life would be like if they existed." Her voice came out deeper, more masculine, and Charlotte squinted at her. If she listened closely she could tell something was off about the voice, like Mary's natural voice hanging just beneath the surface if she listened hard enough.

"That is a good point. The what ifs draw me to penny bloods. Are you using glamour?"

"Yes. It works well in loud, crowded places. Otherwise you have to rely on people not caring enough to look or listen to closely. With all those men at the docks, it wouldn't be safe for ladies dressed like this to be found out, but it would be more unsafe to wander around with them knowing we're ladies." She lifted the necklace. "I modified a rune glamour used to make your voice sound sweeter for ladies bad at singing. I got it from one of Rune Press's books, Practical Uses for Magic in the Home."

"I have that book. It wasn't at all what I was expecting."

"I found it lacking as well. It is a guide for the wealthy who rely on servants to do all the hard work. That causes the book to lack many truly practical uses for magic for the everyday woman."

"Exactly. I can't believe the nobles want to keep their magical knowledge a secret only to waste it on singing and creamy skin."

Mary adjusted the buttons on her shirt. "I heard there are new books coming from Rune Press soon. I'm curious to see what they are. Magicians and commoners have been making better use of magic than the nobles."

"Where are we going exactly?" Margaret asked as she leaned against the doorway, arms crossed over her chest. She was unrecognizable in her loose trousers and shirt. She wore her hat pulled down low, hiding enough of her face to keep her identity hidden. Charlotte rolled up her coat sleeves to keep them from hanging past her hands when she lowered her arms. They all dressed like working men fit for the docks instead of gentleman. Charlotte was grateful for the loose clothing. She didn't think she could hide her chest well enough in a gentleman's suit.

"I'm beginning to think I've been a bad influence on you," Mary chided Margaret.

Charlotte coughed to hide her laugh. The pouts the sisters gave each other were mirrored images.

"If you don't want me to come along then I'll go find a way to give Elizabeth a hard time instead."

"You spend so much time plotting against Elizabeth that I'm growing suspicious of whether or not you truly loathe her as much as you say." Mary arranged a hat on her head.

"She deserves the trouble I give her." Margaret gave the doorway a gentle kick with sole of her boot.

"Or it's an excuse to see her. You can come as long as you promise to not cause us trouble."

"I'll be an angel. Who is our target? I'm afraid I missed that part."

"Bertram Steepe," Charlotte and Mary said in unison.

Margaret grinned. "A Steepe? I love a challenge."

Charlotte felt equally worried and impressed with how well the sisters knew the path to the docks, including the dirty alleys they used as shortcuts. She watched the way they walked and mimicked it, the change in stride uncomfortable at first. The docks were crowded as passengers streamed off one ship and while cargo was loaded and unloaded on the surrounding ones. A forest of ships crowded the water. Birds wheeled above the Thames. The chaos reminded her of the bakery shortly after dawn when the morning rush hit. The rush came with an endless stream of customers in and out the door as the bakery hurried to keep up with the demand.

"Do you know which ship it is?" Mary asked.

All the ships looked the same to Charlotte. The only change was their sizes. "No. Won't the Steepe business name be on it somewhere?"

"I'll go ask before we waste hours looking." Margaret faded into the crowd before her sister could stop her.

"That girl." Mary sighed. "We are going to have to have the talk about not letting ourselves get separated again. I like to dress up to observe, but she enjoys being in the thick of things. It is going to get her into real trouble one day if she isn't careful." She stood up on her tiptoes to search the crowd. "Is there anything specific you think we should look for?"

"I'm interested in the cargo. I want to know what he was hiding in the crate." They stood with their back to a row of carriages, waiting for Margaret to return. "I asked Mr. Steepe if he was familiar with your father's press, and he wasn't. I haven't had a chance to press further. Has there been any interest yet?" She had to raise her voice to be heard over the shouting match happening down the road over the loading of luggage into a carriage. A husband and wife argued as another struggled to fit all her luggage into and onto the carriage.

"No. One other publisher is interested in buying us instead of investing, but they only want a handful of our stories and authors, the most popular ones. Everything else they will drop." Her face creased in pain. "Some of them have great potential if another publisher would wake up enough to see it." She ran her fingers over a hole in her sleeve. "But they want tried and true stories and already recognized names instead of investing in new ones. It is the way of the business, but it pains me to see it happen."

"I understand. I'd be devastated if something happened to the bakery. I've grown used to seeing the same faces week after week. It would be awful to feel like we've let them down." Plenty of them had relied on the bakery for their bread since before she'd been born. To watch the bakery end and not being able to do anything about it would be a nightmare.

Margaret stepped out of the crowd and rejoined them. "The Steepe ship is that large one on the end over there." She pointed to their left. By the time they made it to the ship, the docks had started to empty with passengers streaming away on carriages and dock workers leaving for the day. Sunset lit up the sky in all shades of pink.

"Neither of you happen to know where to find a crowbar, do you?" Charlotte asked as she watched the sailors pile up cargo on the dock. She crossed her arms and glared at a man staring at them as he walked past, a newspaper clutched in his hand. The man turned his head forward. Charlotte grinned. "This is quite freeing."

"There's bound to be a crowbar around here somewhere," Margaret answered, mischief gleaming in her eyes. "Want to crack a few crates open?"

The idea felt dangerous. If they got caught they would get arrested. "Let's." They roamed the area, searching for a crowbar. Then a loud crash shook the dock. A crate tumbled off a stack, the lid popping open as bags spilled out. Margaret scurried toward it with no hesitation, grabbing a bag. The nearest sailor didn't notice until she was already running away.

"Get out of here street rat!" He threw his arms in the air.

She rushed back to them, panting by the time she reached them. "Here you go." She held up the bag, and they all leaned forward. Charlotte held her breath as Margaret prepared to open the bag.

"Is it opium?" Mary asked. "I've heard all kinds of awful stories about the opium dens."

Margaret revealed the tea leaves within and all their shoulders dropped in disappointment.

"Smells like Earl Grey," Charlotte said as she sniffed the bag, the refreshing citrus notes of the bergamot too strong to miss. The smell reminded her of Mr. Steepe.

"Creamy Earl Grey," Mary corrected. "Our father prefers it to regular Earl Grey. He likes the vanilla in it."

"I don't," Margaret said. She leaned to the side and spit on the ground.

Her sister wrinkled her nose. "Really, Margaret. Just because we are pretending to be men doesn't mean we need to act like animals."

"Tell men that. Do you want to open another crate?" Margaret closed the bag.

"We'd have to open them all and there are too many." Mary rubbed between her eyes. "In all honesty I don't even know how to use a crowbar."

Charlotte took the tea from Margaret and squeezed it. "There's nothing hidden inside. Any other ideas?"

"There's a pub nearby," Margaret said. "It can get rough in there, lots of fights, but it is where all the sailors go."

"And why do you know that?" Mary turned a stern eye onto her sister.

Margaret shrugged. "You probably don't want to know."

Mary threw her hands in the air. "We are going to need to have a serious conversation tomorrow. I worry about you."

"Stop worrying. I can look after myself. If Charlotte wants to find information, we could trade the tea for information." She turned back and forth until she decided on the right direction. "Someone might know something if we ask around."

"Or we could buy them a drink and keep the bag." Mary glanced back at the broken crate, but the sailors were already busy moving all the crates away from the docks. "No sense in wasting good tea on those who won't appreciate it."

"Come on then," Margaret urged. "We shouldn't linger too long after dark. I'd rather not have another encounter with a thief on the way home. The last one made off with my pocket watch."

"A broken pocket watch you stole from a potential beau," Mary amended.

"Whether it worked or not isn't the point." Margaret sniffed. "It was a good costume piece." She marched on, leading the way. "The pub will be busy this time of evening. Perfect to ask around."

Sailors and dockworkers crowded the pub. Charlotte couldn't move in any direction without bumping into someone. They weaseled their way into a huddle in the corner of the room. The sour scent of sweat and alcohol clung to the air. "How do we go about asking about the Steepe cargo?"

Both women gave her mischievous smiles. Margaret pointed at a nearby table. "Go on over there and put your foot on the chair and ask if they've seen anything. Forget about being polite. Be aggressive. Act like you don't have time for small talk and have more important places to be."

"And whatever you do, don't apologize," Margaret added. "Women apologize too often."

"Here." Mary took off the necklace and put it around Charlotte's neck.

"How do I sound?" She found it too easy to detect her real voice under the glamour, but Mary gave her an encouraging smile. "Go on and try."

"Shoulders back, walk like you own the place," Margaret whispered while Charlotte faced the table. She threw her shoulders back and sauntered on over to the table. She put her foot up on the empty chair and leaned forward. The men playing cards glanced up at her before returning to their game. "You gents haven't seen any shady happenings that may be connected to a Mr. Steepe, have you?"

"Which one?" A gruff man with a chin full of stubble asked as he laid down a card. "The one who sells the tea or the one in the gun business? Johnny over there unloads their ships." He jutted his thumb at the teen beside him.

"The second one." Although the gun business bit was news to her. It suited him, she thought.

Johnny rubbed his chin. His large clothes hung from his lanky frame. "I've seen a lot of shady dealings, but nothing to do with the Steepes. Except for the street rat trying to steal tea today. An odd thing to steal that."

"Not as strange as the prostitute who loves Johnny here." The gruff man gave the lad's shoulder a squeeze as he cackled. Johnny's expression soured into a scowl. "Don't talk that way about your mother."

The third man hooted and slapped the table. "He's got you there!"

Charlotte backed away from the table. The men barely took notice of her leaving as Johnny slapped down a card that sent the other men cursing.

"Nothing?" Mary asked.

"Nothing."

"Margaret is trying that table over there." Mary pointed to their left.

"Are you going to question anyone?"

Mary shook her head. "No. I'll stick to observing. I prefer to watch than interact."

"Isn't that boring?"

"Not at all. For example, take that man at the end of the bar. See how he keeps looking toward the door and tapping his thumb against the bar? He's probably waiting for someone, but who? I like observing the little day-to-day experiences. Helps me write my own characters and think about how to make them feel human."

"That's a good idea. I need to try that." It must be one of Mary's secrets to making her characters compelling. Like Lord Hollow. As soon as Twilight at Hallow Manor introduced him she couldn't put the story down. She wanted to know more about his mysterious background and habits.

Behind the man at the bar, Margaret argued with a man at a full table. The man flapped his hand in the air at her. Then Margaret ripped the cards out of the large man's hands and slammed them down onto the table. The other three men at the table stood.

"Oh no," Mary said, pressing her hands together. "I should have warned you about Margaret's penchant for starting fights."

Chapter 9

The man whose cards Margaret had revealed jumped to his feet just in time for the man beside him to take a shaky, drunken swing toward Margaret. The punch connected with the side of the first man's jaw, and he went crashing back onto his chair, the wood breaking under him. Charlotte gasped, and Margaret took a step back from the fight.

"We should go." Mary darted forward and grabbed her sister's arm, using it to yank her away from the fight. "What do you think you are doing?" Mary hissed.

"He was cheating! Someone needed to call him on it."

"That isn't our problem."

The large man staggered back onto his feet to grab the man who punched him. He tossed him onto the table, sending cards scattering all over the place. Coins skittered across the worn floorboards. A cup fell, splashing whisky across the floorboards. Heads swiveled to look at all the noise.

"I bet the large man wins," Charlotte said, caught up in the excitement. She kept glancing back to keep track of the fight's progress.

"I wouldn't be so sure," Margaret said as she bent down to pick up a half penny that bumped into her boot. "All that muscle tires a man like that out too much in a fight. Someone fast and light on their feet can take advantage of that."

"Then which one are you betting on?" Charlotte shoved her hands into her pockets to keep from clapping in delight as a smaller man jumped onto the first man's back. Seeing a brawl was better than reading about one. As the large man flailed about, unable to get the other man off his back, she thought Margaret might be right about the winner.

"We should get out of here before this gets out of hand." Mary pulled them both toward the door. The large man turned, falling backward onto the table beside them to pin the smaller man down.

"But I want to know who wins," Margaret protested.

"Me too," Charlotte said.

Mary let out an exasperated huff. "We are here to find out about Bertram Steepe's dark secrets, not bet on pub brawls."

Chastened, Charlotte nodded. "Right. It's hard not to get caught up in the moment." Mary was right. None of them could afford to get pulled into the fight. The harsh bite of reality let fear trickle in. Charlotte didn't know how to punch let alone defend herself against a man stronger than she was. Somewhere to their left a glass smashed as a man let out a war cry.

Then an explosion rocked the air. The windows rattled. Everyone in the pub froze. A bell rang and all at once the fight was forgotten as men rushed outside. Mary kept a tight grip on Charlotte and Margaret as they followed the tide outside. Smoke curled up into the air off the Steepes' ship. The mast hung crooked and a gaping hole in the side almost reached the waterline.

"Is that shady enough for you?" Margaret asked. She grinned as she took off running toward the ship. Mary and Charlotte struggled to keep up with her. The warehouse and now the ship, it had to be more than a coincidence, but Charlotte couldn't figure out what the aim could be. Away from the men rushing for the ship, a lone figure ran away from the docks. Like at the warehouse, the figure wore a suit, but in the gloom of twilight she couldn't make out the details of his face.

"Over there!" Charlotte changed course. If she moved quick enough she could cut the man off, but his legs were longer than hers, his steps larger. She couldn't keep up with his breakneck pace. The gap between them grew with each step. He reached a carriage and dove inside it.

"Stop!" Charlotte yelled. The carriage driver didn't listen. The carriage pulled away, carrying the man farther and farther out of reach. She huffed, reaching out for the carriage and chasing it a few steps before giving up and doubling over, resting her hands on her knees as she huffed and puffed. Mary fared no better. She came up behind Charlotte a few seconds later gasping for breath.

"I'm not a runner," she said as she sat down on an empty crate.

Charlotte straightened. "What are you sitting on?"

"A box I think." Mary glanced down. "Yes, a box."

Charlotte ushered her off and turned the crate over, peering inside. That same acrid, metallic smell from Bertram's package made her nose twitch. The lid lay on the ground, the top sporting the same cracks too.

"I saw Bertram with this package the other day. This is what he wanted brought to the docks instead of Mr. Steepe's house. I think the man we were chasing was Bertram."

"Do you think that means he caused the explosion?"

"He may have planted something on the ship, but it's my understanding that both he and Martin use it. I don't see why he'd go after his own ship."

"I thought those crates were only tea." Mary rested her hands on her hips as she caught her breath. "Could it be an insurance scheme?"

"Maybe, but I don't see how that could be worthwhile if he is hurting his business. Unless ..." Men crawled over the ship like ants. The cloud of smoke drifted away on the wind. A yell went up and men scattered, the creaking mast splitting the air as it fell closer to the water.

"Unless what?"

"Unless he doesn't mean to hurt his business, but his cousin's. Though I can't see why he'd take the risk, not when the last fire only hurt Bertram."

Margaret finally caught up to them, holding aloft a piece of jagged wood like a trophy. "I found a memento from the ship. Everyone was saying the explosion must be sabotage."

"A memento wasn't necessary," Mary said.

"No, but I wanted one. It'll make for a great story to tell people."

"This confirms he is up to something, but without proof it doesn't help me." Charlotte inspected the crate again. Nothing linked it to Bertram. She could be imagining things, desperate to hit back at the man causing her grief. And in the end he was right. She was a mere commoner and her courtship was doomed. She'd had her chance to confess and hadn't. Mr. Steepe would be right to be cross with her when Bertram told him the truth.

"We should get out of here." Mary shifted on her feet, glancing about. "If the bobbies start questioning witnesses, we'll be found out. I hear trained investigators are good at spotting glamour."

Margaret tucked the chunk of wood under her arm. "Father wouldn't be happy if we got arrested. Especially you. You're supposed to be the good one."

"I can't imagine why when I'm not the one sneaking out of the house at night. Don't think I don't hear you climbing out the window. The last thing I want is for you to wind up kidnapped by an opium den. You are tempting trouble to get you."

Margaret shoved her hands into her pockets and headed down the road, expression glum. "Since when did this mission become about me? Did Charlotte find what she needed?"

"No." Charlotte squeezed the bag of tea in her pocket. She felt guilty for taking it. "I think Bertram was the cause of the explosion, but I have no way to prove it. And with no proof, I have nothing to use against him." There was nothing she could do to keep Bertram from telling on her. Perhaps she deserved it after not coming clean right away.

"Maybe you don't need proof," Mary suggested.

"What do you mean?" Charlotte fell in step beside her while they followed Margaret's quick pace.

"There is a serial I've been reading about a detective similar to The Boy Detective. He wound up in a similar situation with no physical proof, but plenty of coincidences and eye witnesses. He pretended he had evidence to get the villain to confess."

Charlotte considered the idea. Leading Bertram into a trap would be her only option with no proof. A tabby cat yowled and darted across the road in front of them, sending Charlotte's heart racing. The earlier thrill of the brawl seeped out of her, fear creeping in with how menacing the dark streets looked. A thief could hide around any corner and they wouldn't see them. They avoided the alleyways this time as they huddled close together. All the stories of murder and theft too close.

"I don't know if such a tactic would work, but it may be all I have," she said, trying to focus on her problem to keep the growing fear at bay.

"Is Martin Steepe worth fighting over?" Margaret asked. "He's just a man. There are plenty of those around."

"Not enough rich ones willing to court the likes of us," Mary said.

Charlotte threw her hands up. "Why does everyone insist on reminding me of his money? There is more to a happy marriage than money."

"Sure," Mary said. "But a lot of money helps. That's why all the love interests in popular romances are rich. There is a special kind of comfort to knowing you don't need to worry about your next meal or the roof over your head."

Margaret nodded. "If I have to marry and put up with a man, he'd better have enough money to make it worth my while."

Charlotte smiled at the sincerity to Margaret's words. "Martin is sweet despite his lack of social grace. And I like what he is doing with his own press. Making magic available to all is an honorable cause, and it is one less thing the nobles can hoard to themselves. I wouldn't mind getting to be a part of that."

Mary sighed. "You're falling in love, how romantic."

Charlotte stammered. Was she falling in love? The thought of Bertram getting his way made her stomach twist and pang with anger. "I wouldn't go as far as to say it's love. More like I'm starting to like him after our unusual first meeting. I like the idea of what could be." None of her attempts at past courtships got very far. Most of the men remained uninterested in marrying yet, or quickly became enamored with someone else. None of them had given her the growing attention Mr. Steepe gave her.

A drunk stumbled down the street singing a sea chantey. "'Ey, lads. Want to get a drink with me?" he called out as they passed by.

Margaret's steps slowed, and Mary grabbed her to haul her onward. Charlotte huddled closer to them as long shadows wavered in the light of a lantern in an alleyway. She couldn't breathe easy until they stepped back inside Mary's house. Margaret crept off to her own room, Mary hissing behind her that she'd better not try to sneak out.

"I'm sorry we couldn't find more," Mary said as she straightened her dress. "I do hope that villain doesn't change Mr. Steepe's mind about you."

Charlotte slipped back into her dress, the familiarity of being back in her own clothes putting her at ease. As freeing as the costume had been, nothing could match the comfort of her own identity. "It can't be helped." There wasn't much to lose if she made a fool of herself. Only her fiancé, her chance to be published by Hawke, and her dignity. She hoped she wouldn't have to fake another faint.

"Would you like to stay in our spare room tonight? I'd hate to see you go out alone at this time of night."

"If you don't mind, I'd appreciate it. Going home this late would wake up my parents and I hate to interrupt their sleep with how early they rise."

Mary leaned forward. "Want to see an early copy of the serials that we'll be publishing tomorrow?"

"Yes I would," Charlotte said, her eyes widening at the prospect. "Which ones do you have?"

"All of them, including the next chapter of mine. It's a rather tense chapter for Lord Hallow."

"I hate to interrupt your reading," Margaret said as she crept out of her room, keeping her voice to a whisper. "But there is a man standing across the street watching our house."

Mary paused. "Watching our house? Are you sure?"

"He was standing out there staring at the house. What else would he be doing?"

"Let me see."

They all shuffled into Margaret's room, leaving the candle in the hallway to avoid giving their presence away. Outside the street was empty.

Margaret pressed her face against the window. "He was there a minute ago! He looked right at me when I looked out."

"Probably just someone passing through or leaving the tavern late," Mary soothed as she rubbed Margaret's back. She shot Charlotte a worried look.

"What if it was a vampire?" Margaret said, yanking her curtains shut.

"Vampires aren't real. The excitement of the night is getting to you is all. Keep your curtains shut and all will be well. And don't sneak out."

"I won't," Margaret grumbled.

"Do you want to come read with us?"

"No thank you. I'm going to bed." Margaret shooed them out.

Charlotte wanted to agree with Mary's assessment of the situation, but unease prickled down her neck. "Do you think it has to do with our time at the docks?"

"I don't know," Mary said. "It could be nothing at all."

"Maybe you have an admirer," Charlotte suggested as they headed downstairs to the parlor.

"I've never had a real admirer. Most of them have been authors trying to get into my uncle's good graces and would call on me as an excuse to see him."

"Men. They can be despicable, can't they?"

"Indeed." Mary peeked out the curtains in the parlor before readjusting them. "Let me fetch the papers. We have a new story that starts with this issue. Whether it continues or not depends on how the situation with the company plays out, but I rather like the adventure."

Charlotte curled up in a chair. But even Lord Hallow's tragic backstory couldn't keep her gaze from darting toward the windows. The watching man felt like too much a coincidence after their trip to the docks.

Chapter 10

S he wore her thick hair pinned up in the back in a stylish bun, cushioning the back of her head from the carriage wall each time the carriage hit a pothole that sent her bouncing in her seat. She balled her lavender skirt in her hands. Not wanting to show up in the same dress she already fainted once in, she'd had no choice but to pay to have this dress modified to make it fashionable again. She bet Mr. Steepe's mother never needed to worry about being out of fashion and not having enough dresses for social functions. The woman likely had far more dresses than Charlotte and her mother combined.

The carriage rolled to a stop, and the coachman opened the door and helped her out. The sight of the manor made her nerves explode as her palms sweat and her chest tightened. She didn't feel ready for this dinner. Didn't think she ever would. She couldn't shake the feeling this dinner would be the end of her engagement at long last.

Laoise met her at the door. "I overheard Mr. Steepe's cousin asking the stable boy about your address." Laoise lifted a finger into the air. "Very clever getting dropped off and picked up at the bookstore."

"It isn't clever. My mother is convinced this engagement will end in a wedding and I need time to myself to breathe." She glanced around Laoise. "Please tell me I'm not late." The voices coming from the parlor were too faint for her to identify. A white streak ran through the entryway and toward the back of the house, its collar jingling. She did a double take. The creature looked like a rabbit, but its body was far too long to be a rabbit.

"What was that?" Charlotte asked, voice shrill.

"What was what?" Laoise looked about.

"The thing that just ran through here." She pointed ahead.

Laoise turned, but they were alone. "The jingling? That would be Oolong. Mr. Steepe gave him a collar with a bell this week after Bertram tripped over him twice in one visit. If you hear the bell coming your way, watch where you are walking. He loves to get underfoot."

"I don't think ... never mind." She glanced back at where the creature had gone, but there was no sign of it. She was more stressed than she realized if she was imagining strange rabbits. For all she knew it could be another one of Bertram's plots to discredit her, like with his cinnamon buns. She'd be the mad baker's daughter who saw rabbits everywhere.

Laoise pointed toward the parlor. "The Steepe family is waiting for you in there." She waggled her eyebrows. "Make Mr. Steepe faint this time."

"Laoise," Charlotte hissed. Laoise cast her a faux look of wide-eyed innocence.

Charlotte refused to give herself any time for second guessing and more worrying. She charged toward the parlor. When Charlotte entered the room, Mrs. Steepe laughed at something Bertram said, patting him on the arm with affection. Martin's gaze caught on Charlotte, a wide smile breaking across his face as he stood.

"Miss Graham!" He approached her, and she curtsied to him. He stopped mid-stride to offer a bow. Charlotte bit her bottom lip to keep from giggling at how serious he looked whenever he bowed.

"There is no need to bow," Bertram muttered.

"Hello, Mr. Steepe."

"Please, let's do away with the formalities. Call me Martin."

"Then call me Charlotte."

"Miss Graham," Bertram said as he joined them. He dropped his voice. "I was starting to worry you wouldn't come." She searched for the same feeling of freedom she'd felt when she put on the clothes of a man and the rush that came later in the pub when she didn't feel the pressure to be polite. She lifted a hand to her mouth. "Oh, have I troubled you? I apologize. I got carried away looking for Martin's books at my favorite bookstore."

"How darling," Mrs. Steepe said, her voice sounding authentic. "I always do the same. I can't help myself, I'm too proud."

Martin gave his mother an affectionate look. "You are Rune Press's most ardent supporter."

Betram looked away, hiding his expression.

"I'm not late, am I?" Charlotte asked.

"You are not late at all," Martin assured her. "You are right on time. Please allow me to escort you into the dining room." He offered her his arm, and she took it. Inside the dining room he halted as he took in the place setting at the head of the table. "Is father home early?"

"No, dear, I thought you should have his place while he is gone. He helped Charlotte to her seat before stopping at his chair. He laid a hand on the back of the chair, looking down at it with reverence. Then finally he sat.

"Shall I light the candles?" the butler asked.

"Only one. I'll light the rest myself. I have been working on a new piece of magic I'd like to try out."

"Shall I get a bucket of water?"

"Not this time."

Charlotte gripped the armrests, watching as the butler lit a single candle and handed it to Martin.

"Thank you." Martin stood. He mumbled a string of words Charlotte didn't understand as his fingers traced the runes in the wax. And then he blew on the candle. The flame sputtered and then half of it broke away, floating on to the next candle. The flame continued on until it reached the last candle, lighting each each one it passed. His mother clapped. Charlotte joined in. Martin bowed before retaking his seat.

"Will dinner be ready soon?" Bertram asked.

"I'll check," Mrs. Steepe said. "I'm going to take a look at our wine options as well." Her heels clicked against the hardwood floor as she left.

Bertram's jaw tensed as he turned a steely gaze to Charlotte. "I take it your parents were unable to attend?"

"They are away visiting my aunt." She refused to look at him, afraid she would give the lie away if she did.

"Perhaps next time," Martin said. "I would love to meet them."

"They are gone for the summer, unfortunately."

"I'm sure they could return early to meet your fiancé," Bertram said, quirking one eyebrow. A maid poured them all glasses of wine. Bertram swished the glass and took a small sip.

"They can't." Her mind spun as she searched for an excuse. "They are afraid to travel after ... after a highwayman held up their carriage."

Bertram snorted into his wine glass. "Don't tell me it was Dick Turpin."

"Ghastly!" Martin shifted in his seat, fingers tapping on the table in worry. "I didn't know we had highwaymen still rampaging through the countryside. Someone should really catch this Mr. Turpin."

"I think they already did." Bertram stared Charlotte down over the rim of his cup.

"Thank goodness," Martin said. "I hope your parents will have a safe return trip."

"I do as well." Charlotte gave him a strained smile. "How has business been?" she asked, desperate to change the subject.

"Excellent," Martin replied. "The shop has gone well enough for me to focus on preparations to showcase my teas for The Great Exhibition later this year." Devised by Prince Albert, the exhibition would display the works of industry and magic from across the world. Charlotte had forgotten all about it, too caught up in her delicate engagement with Mr. Steepe. "Bertie, are you still on track with the fundraising we discussed for the Steepe Foundation?"

"Yes. Better than expected in fact. I have a party in two days and I hope to have the rest of the funds secured there."

"Steepe Foundation? What is that?" Charlotte asked. "I'm afraid I'm not familiar."

Martin finished sipping on his wine before responding. "We donate to causes that help children, and we help fund a school for the poor. We are currently raising funds to get the roof repaired and hire another teacher. Bertram and our mothers handle most of the foundation work."

Bertram peered over the top of his wine glass. "Yes. Martin offended a few ladies when he misremembered their names. He also doesn't get enough social invites to secure enough donations. He focuses on the numbers and suppliers for us instead."

Martin frowned. "I didn't mean to misremember their names, but you are far better than I at socializing. We've hit every financial goal so far because of you. No one is better at fundraising than you, and I wouldn't dare hope to compete."

"I do what I can," Bertram said, sounding bored.

Mrs. Steepe returned, declaring dinner was on its way. Seconds later two maids stepped into the room with trays of food. Charlotte's mouth watered at the smell of roast beef. A maid put a plate down in front of her. Charlotte admired the artfully arranged meal. Her meals at home seemed plain in comparison. The food was as delicious as it smelled, the tender beef like butter in her mouth. The busy bakery often meant their daytime meals were rushed as they stuck to simple recipes.

"Auntie, wouldn't it be wonderful if Miss Graham's parents joined us next time if they return from her aunt's house in time?"

"Of course. I'd be happy to host the full Graham family." Suspicion shone in her eyes, but unlike Bertram she didn't push.

"What does your father do? I don't think I've had the pleasure of meeting him before." The smug smile he gave her left Charlotte longing to throw her plate at him.

"Unfortunately they won't be returning soon as I said earlier. You'll have to wait."

"Ah, yes. Such a shame about the highwayman attacking them," he drawled. He shoved a forkful of potatoes into his mouth. His expression told her he was savoring every bite.

"Highwayman?" Mrs. Steepe's head rose, her fork paused.

"Apparently Mr. and Mrs. Graham got held up recently," Bertram explained. "Isn't that right, Miss Graham?" He drew out the "miss."

"I would be more than happy to escort them back myself," Martin offered.

"That is sweet, thank you, but please don't worry about them. They'll be fine. Personally, I've been worried about the explosion at the docks last night. It's in all the papers this morning. How awful for it to have been a Steepe ship. Do you know what happened?"

"Not yet. The investigation is still going." Martin cut a forkful of meat, not seeming the least bit concerned about the topic.

"An unfortunate accident I'm sure. Nothing you need to worry yourself about," Bertram added, his fork stabbing at a slice of roast beef.

"But I heard that witnesses saw someone dressed like a gentleman run away from the scene." She put on her best innocent expression.

Bertram's fork stilled.

"Who do you think it could have been? A competitor? Someone close to Martin?"

Bertram set his fork down and took a long sip of wine. "I hope you are not implying you think it could have been sabotage."

"I'm merely wondering if I should be worried. If someone is trying to hurt Martin, I want to know."

Mrs. Steepe nodded. "Understandable. I would feel the same if I worried someone were targeting my husband, but Martin assured me no tea was lost in the explosion."

"What good news," Bertram said, voice strained. He cleared his throat. "See? Nothing to worry about."

"Well, that isn't entirely true." Martin's face was somber as he leaned back in his chair.

"What do you mean?" Bertram stiffened.

"I was going to wait until after dinner." He shifted in his seat and took a sip of tea.

"Martin." Bertram's voice came out sharp.

"I'm afraid that while all my tea had already been unloaded, your new rifle prototype was still on the ship and has been lost."

Bertram squeezed his fork, his knuckles turning white. "My prototype wasn't due to arrive for another two weeks."

"There was plenty of space on my recent shipment and since there was no rush I asked the captain to stop in France and get it for you. I know how hard you've been working on the design this past year. I thought I would surprise you by getting it to you early." He spun his teacup, mouth twitching as though he didn't know whether to frown or smile to comfort Bertram. "I'm sorry, Bertie. I didn't know the ship would explode."

Bertram's face turned red. He dropped his fork and stood. His mouth opened, his gaze jumping between Martin and his aunt. His mouth flapped, but no words came out. Then he ran for the front door, his heavy footsteps echoing through the house.

Martin winced. "Forgive him. This is rather bad news for him. I will give him time to calm down and then see if there is anything I can do tomorrow." He sighed. "I feel awful about it."

"It's not your fault," Mrs. Steepe said as she refilled his teacup. "You had good intentions and didn't know. I'm sure Bertram will see that."

"Either way, I wish the ship hadn't exploded. Bertram may not be able to get a new prototype finished in time for the grand opening of The Great Exhibition. He's had such a terrible run of bad luck lately." He shook his head in pity.

"As long as he has you to help him he will be fine."

Martin tapped his fingers against his fork in thought. "I will continue to remind him he is family. I fear he has felt out of sorts ever since Father officially made me his heir."

Charlotte grasped onto that. "Was Bertram originally the heir?"

Mrs. Steepe returned to her food, slicing off a bite of beef. "Martin was ill as a child. Until Martin was fourteen, Bertram attended parties and work meetings in his place. Martin was a voracious learner with a hungry mind, but he wasn't well enough to train at his father's side." Her eyes went distant, her mouth twitching. "It was a difficult time and Bertram thought he would need to continue to act as heir for the sake of the family. He has several sisters himself he helps support."

"Which one of you is older?" Charlotte asked.

"He's several years older than me," Martin said, worrying his napkin between his fingers. "I'm glad his investments have gone so well. He didn't seem to know what to do with himself at first once I finally stepped up. I don't personally see the appeal of rifles, but they've done well enough for him."

"But this is a dreary topic," Mrs. Steepe said, cutting off small bites. "Let's talk about something lighter. Did your new tea come from China yet?"

Martin's face brightened. "It did. Perhaps we can try it after dinner."

"I'm sure Charlotte would love to, but I plan to check on the garden after dinner." Mrs. Steepe took a bite of the roasted vegetables.

"Your gardens are beautiful," Charlotte said. "I've never been able to grow anything, but my mother used to grow daisies."

Mrs. Steepe smiled. "When she visits I will share my daisies with her."

"She would love that." With Bertram gone, Charlotte attacked her meal with gusto. She tried to picture her mother at the table and how thrilled she'd be with all the food. Her parents would look out of place at the Steepe's dining table. They'd look more like the servants, but her father could probably go toe-to-toe with Martin when it came to business talk, at least certain aspects of it. Charlotte too, for that matter, but discussing profits didn't seem like a good courtship topic.

When they finished, Mrs. Steepe rose. "Martin, why don't you go fetch your new tea while I walk Miss Graham to the parlor."

"Grand idea." Martin set off and Mrs. Steepe gestured for Charlotte to come with her.

Charlotte balled her hands. If she wanted any hope of a real engagement, she needed to impress Mrs. Steepe.

"Thank you for dining with us. Martin has been looking forward to dinner all day," Mrs. Steepe said.

"I appreciate the invitation. The food was wonderful."

Mrs. Steepe rested a hand on Charlotte's arm, stopping her in the entrance to the parlor. "I'm going to get right to it. I want you to know that whatever family scandal you are trying to hide, you have no need to fear. We are no strangers to gossip and know better than to put too much stock into it. My aunt married into the Hammond family and has caused plenty of shock over the years. Did you know she has twelve dachshunds?"

Charlotte shivered at the reminder. "I'm aware. I've met a few of them."

"Why at one of her luncheons this poor girl wound up in tears after … Oh I can't bear to recount the tale. It's too awful." Mrs. Steepe squinted at her. Charlotte squeezed her hands tighter, hoping Mrs. Steepe didn't recognize her from that dreadful party. "Martin is a sweet boy with a kind heart, but he is simply a wooden spoon when it comes to social niceties. It was his sickness you see." She pressed her lips together as she turned toward the family portrait. "It kept him home for several years where he was far too isolated. Be patient with him instead of assuming the worst. And please, don't break his heart like his last fiancée."

"His other fiancée ..." Charlotte started, trying to think of the most tactful way to ask what happened to her, "wh—"

Mrs. Steepe looked over Charlotte's shoulder, mouth and eyes widening in terror. She screamed, the sound loud and shrill. Charlotte whirled around, finding a large, monstrous rabbit running at them. Its gait was all wrong on its overly long body. Its tongue lolled out of its mouth.

Charlotte screamed too, and then the creature was upon her legs, her doom sealed.

Chapter 11

The rabbit jumped up, his front paws on her legs while its slimy, rough tongue licked her hand. She leaned away, trying to escape the nightmarish creature. Mrs. Steepe stumbled back until she fell into a chair with a gasp. The rabbit let out a low whuff, ears twitching. It turned its gaze on Mrs. Steepe before deciding to go in for another lick on Charlotte's hands. She pulled both hands out of reach. The rabbit let out another whuff.

"Nooo!" Charlotte moaned while she waved her hands to shoo the rabbit away.

"What's wrong?" Martin called out.

His mother let out a strangled cry for help.

A second later he rounded the corner and stepped into the room. His cross expression landed on the rabbit. "Oolong! I've told you no climbing or jumping on guests." The rabbit fell back onto all fours and ran to Martin, ears flapping.

"What is that ... that thing?" Mrs. Steepe shuddered as the rabbit's tongue lolled out.

"It's just Oolong. Charlotte once had an unfortunate run in with some dachshunds, and so I thought making Oolong look like a cute bunny would help her warm up to him I just ..." He held out his hands as if measuring something and then moved them closer together. "I haven't figured out how to make him look shorter yet. None of the glamour books for ladies had any tips on the problem. They seem more concerned with making things bigger, not smaller." Martin bent down to pet the beast, and it wiggled in delight. Then it fell onto its side and rolled onto its back.

She felt silly for not realizing it was the dog, but with his proportions all wrong it was hard to focus on anything else. She averted her gaze, unable to bear the sight. "I appreciate the gesture, truly, but until you perfect the glamour I think it may be best to leave it off. He is too long for a rabbit."

Martin undid Oolong's collar, and the glamour fell away. "I meant to keep him away from dinner but he scurried off when I got the tea."

"Please warn me next time before you glamour the dog." Mrs. Steepe rose on shaking legs. "I'm going to go see to the garden. I need a moment to myself." Mrs. Steepe left, a hand pressed to her chest, face pale.

Charlotte did appreciate the thought, but she didn't want to think of which animal he might try next. A cat? A mini horse? Nothing would fit Oolong's proportions right. Charlotte threw her shoulders back and kneeled down. For Martin, she thought. She would pet the dog before he got any other ideas on how to help with her fear of dogs and gave her new creatures to fear in the process. "Oolong."

The dog's ears perked up. She called for him again and he rolled back onto his feet and trotted over to her, his tongue inside his mouth this time. He sank onto his belly in front of her, letting out a groan as she scratched his head. "How old is he really? I mean, you said you've had the same dog since you were a boy but surely a dog can't live that long." She watched him, waiting for his reaction.

He chuckled as he took a seat. "Of course they aren't the same dog. He's not one year old yet. My mother got me my second dog when the first died and she didn't have the heart to tell me. She hoped if she got me a new dog I wouldn't figure it out, but of course I did right away. However, I didn't want to break her heart and went along with the ruse."

"And you continued the naming scheme?"

"Yes. It makes it easy to remember their names. The familiarity is comforting and easy to remember. I made sure to name each one after a different oolong tea. Don Cong is a phoenix tea, and I thought the name fitting since he reminds me so much of my first dog. Did you have any pets growing up?"

"No, but I did sneak a stray cat into my room once." It'd been Laoise's idea and her habit for trouble as a child. "I got found out right away because my father is allergic. The cat hair on my clothes sent him into a sneezing fit as soon as he saw me."

Laoise carried a tea set and a kettle full of water into the room, steam drifting from the spout. She set it on the coffee table. "Anything else I can get you, Mr. Steepe?" The sweet voice she put on reminded Charlotte of how Laoise spoke to Charlotte's parents.

"Tea is all. Thank you, Shannon."

Laoise didn't react to the name, making Charlotte wonder how often he called her that. As Laoise passed behind him, she pointed at him and made a kissing face. Charlotte glared at her.

"Shannon," she said, emphasizing the name in the sweetest voice she could manage, "can you bring me a slice of trifle from tonight's dessert?"

Laoise glared back. "Of course, my lady." She gave her an exaggerated curtsy.

"Make that two," Martin added. "I haven't had mine yet either."

"Right away, sir." Laoise left, casting one last pointed glare over her shoulder at Charlotte.

Charlotte moved back to her seat. Martin scooted his chair closer to hers. The closeness gave her a whiff of his bergamot cologne and a thriller tingled through her at how close they were. Charlotte heated up the water back to the optimal temperature, taking care to get the runes right this time. The stem thickened, and she sat back, satisfied in her handiwork. Oolong threw himself across Martin's feet, looking tired out after his adventure as a rabbit.

"That really is a useful spell. With some tweaking I bet I could use it on teapots to keep the tea hot." His forehead wrinkled as he considered the idea. "It would make a great product for my store and a great addition to my self-pouring teapots." His gaze turned distant as he mulled over the idea. His fingers tapped against the armrests, his arm twitching.

Worried she'd lost him to his business musings, Charlotte spoke up to reel him back to the present. "What tea are we having?"

Martin jerked back to attention. "Golden Monkey. I just got it in on the last shipment." He spooned the tea leaves into the teapot before continuing. "It is from China. In the past only the wealthy had access to this tea. They believed it can increase sexual virility."

Charlotte pressed her lips together to keep her giggle in. Coming from anyone else she would have taken his words as a hint.

"It proved to be more difficult than I anticipated to get my hands on it let alone enough of it to sell. I'm glad it came in time for me to share it with you." He beamed at her.

Warmth spread through Charlotte's chest. She held on to that feeling of being wanted. Heavens knew she would miss it when all this ended. "I'm glad I get to try it too."

Laoise returned with a dessert tray. Oolong lifted his head as she set the food down. She left and his head drooped back to the floor.

Charlotte grabbed her trifle and tasted a small bite, letting the flavors linger on her tongue. "Is that orange I taste?" She reached for the little notebook she liked to carry with her. After patting both sides she remembered she hadn't been able to bring it. She usually carried it around in her apron and without her apron, no notebook.

"Did you lose something?"

"I was looking for my notebook. I like to write down desserts I enjoy. Then I can recreate the recipes or take inspiration for new ones." With her mind unable to focus on a new book, recipes were the next best thing. They wouldn't satisfy her for long, but at least they kept her mind busy with a creative outlet in the meantime.

Martin pulled a little notebook from his pocket. "Would you like to borrow mine?"

Her mouth opened in surprise. "You carry around a notebook too?"

"Yes, but I take notes on teas. I bring this with me to all tea tastings and business meetings. The notes help me decide what to sell and keep track of ideas for my own blends. Helps me keep track of other business matters too."

"You don't mind letting me borrow it?" Her fingers itched to get a hold of the notebook. To get a peek into his mind.

"Of course not." He handed it to her along with an enchanted quill, the magic ghosting over her fingers. "Do you often take notes?"

"All the time. I like to make my own creations. The only desserts I like more than fruity ones are chocolate sweets."

The teapot poured the tea. Her attention caught on the inviting stream of steam curling up into the air as she considered all the flavor notes of the trifle. She took another bite, this time the vanilla in the pudding popped on her tongue. She murmured to herself as she wrote, sorting through all the flavors while Martin watched her. When her scribbling ended, Martin spoke up.

"Are you planning on making it?"

"Not quite this one, but I'm thinking a similar version where chocolate and oranges are the main component."

"That sounds wonderful," he murmured.

She put the trifle down and reached for her tea. "Should I add cream or honey to this?"

"No. Golden Monkey is best black."

She took a tentative sip. The tea was smooth with a tasting note that reminded her of peaches. "That is good."

"It is considered one of the best black teas in the world. Well worth the hefty price." He raised his teacup as if in a toast to her before taking a sip.

She took another taste of the tea and then another bite of trifle. Martin crossed his legs at the ankle. She put the notebook down on the stand beside her, moving aside the book sitting there. Wuthering Heights. "Your mother's I presume?"

"Yes. I haven't read that one, but she adores it. Have you read it?"

"No. Too sad for my tastes."

"Then what do you like to read?"

"I'm currently reading Twilight at Hallow Manor." It was a romance at heart more than a horror. Surely it wouldn't scare him off like the grisly crime stories she liked. "It's a Hawke House serial. Have you read it?"

"No, unfortunately." He shifted, embarrassment making his hands twitch. "But I will look for it next time I'm out shopping."

"Please do. It is my favorite story from Hawke."

"Do you have any other favorites?"

"Of course, but I don't think they are good topics for conversation." He'd need to know her reading tastes eventually, just like he'd need to know she was a baker's daughter. She couldn't be with a man who didn't appreciate a good blood penny.

"Why heavens not?"

"My favorite is, well gruesome. It is nothing at all like Wuthering Heights."

"What is the title? You have me too curious."

"The String of Pearls. There is a play based on it."

He gave her a sad smile. "I don't know that one either, but I will look for it. Please write it down in my notebook for me as a reminder."

A low whistle echoed from somewhere in the bowels of the house. Oolong rolled onto his feet and took off so quickly his feet slid in place for a few steps before he found traction. He headed toward the kitchen. Then a moment later a crash echoed through the house followed by a bark.

Martin frowned. "Oh dear. I should have put his collar back on him. I fear the butler may quit if he trips on Oolong one more time."

"You make Oolong sound like quite the troublemaker." She stuffed another bite of trifle into her mouth, picking apart all the flavors and how they played together. The orange blended well into the vanilla sponge cake and pudding.

Martin waved his hands as he spoke. "He doesn't mean to be. He is easily excitable is all and prefers to run instead of walk. And because he is short, he has a habit of sneaking up on people without his bell."

As if he'd heard his name, Oolong came running back into the room, skidding to a stop in front of Martin. He slid across the floor until he bumped into the chair. Then he sat down, tongue lolling out of his mouth.

"Better to be safe until I put the other collar back on you." Martin leaned down and put the collar on Oolong. The air shimmered around the dog and then he turned back into the nightmarish rabbit. He flopped down and let out a groan as his eyes shut. "There. No more sneaking up on anyone."

"I think I am starting to warm up to him. At least, he doesn't frighten me anymore." Nothing could be more terrifying than his appearance as a rabbit. In comparison, the normal Oolong looked far more pleasant.

Martin squinted at Charlotte. She paused, wondering what was wrong. Then he leaned forward, stopping less than a hand's width away from her face. A kiss already? She hadn't expected one this soon, not that she had any complaints. His lips looked inviting, that citrus scent of his pulling her in. She swallowed and tilted her head up. Her heart raced as much from nerves as excitement. She began to lean toward him but his hand came up, wiping at the corner of her mouth with his finger. "A spot of cream, but I got it."

She sank back into her chair, disappointment rushing through her. He leaned back and dug into his slice of trifle. "This has been such a nice evening. I'm glad you came. Would you attend a party with me next month? A magician I do business with is hosting a garden party. Everyone invites Bertram to parties, but not me. I try not to miss any I'm invited to."

"I'd love to attend with you." She smiled, tickled at the invitation. It'd been far too long since she had gotten to dance. The thought of dancing with Martin made her warm in giddiness. "There will be dancing, right? I'd like to dance."

His twitching hands stilled. "Then we shall dance as much as you wish."

As much as she wished! No man had ever said that to her before. "I'll look forward to dancing you right off your feet."

He gave her a boyish smile, his hand reaching out for hers. His fingers brushed over hers, the delicate touch sending goose bumps over her skin. "I will look forward to being danced off my feet."

The way he looked at her and the husky tone in his voice, it was all too much. Mrs. Steepe had been wrong to ask Charlotte to not break his heart. If anyone's heart was going to be broken it was hers when he discovered the truth about her identity.

She hoped that day never came.

Chapter 12

Another party meant another new dress. Hers were too worn and faded to hold up to a society party and no amount of tweaking could save them.

"You will look great in the dress. The color reminds me of honey and it looks good against your dark hair," Mary said as they left the shop. They passed a man leaning against the shop, newspaper in front of his face. "You have every reason to be optimistic."

Laoise hadn't been able to come. She'd wanted to spend the day with her brother. The latest bout of illness had come upon him in full force. Charlotte refrained from begging, knowing if one of her family were sick she'd want to be with them too.

She wanted to be optimistic about her own situation, but all she could think about was how much lighter her purse felt after paying for the new dress. She'd have to give up buying her serials for the next few months. The last thing she wanted to do was drain her parents dry of money in a failed courtship attempt. "It feels like everything could get pulled out from under me."

"That's exactly why you need optimism. Focus on the good instead of letting your fears win out." Mary glanced down the busy road. It felt like everyone had the same idea as them to get outside and take advantage of the beautiful weather. Young ladies roved in pairs and packs up and down the street as they shopped. "Want to walk to the park? It's close by and your beau's tea shop is on the way."

"I forgot about his shop." Charlotte smacked her forehead. "I should visit." And buy something to make up for the tea they stole.

They passed two women Charlotte recognized. The tailor's daughters. She murmured a greeting to them that they returned. But as soon as they passed by the women snickered. Charlotte's face warmed. The snickers had to be about the Hammond Dachshund incident. Those two had been in attendance and were vicious gossips.

Mary shifted her sun umbrella. "The shop is that one right down there with the black awning." She pointed ahead. "They carry teas I've never heard of before. I like browsing the shelves and reading the trivia scattered around the store."

"I've been impressed by his tea so far. Although I feel a little bad about taking that bag from the docks."

"He won't miss one bag I'm sure." Mary opened the door to the shop, waving for Charlotte to go first. Mary lingered at the door a moment before stepping in behind her. Mary took a deep breath. "I wish I could bottle up this scent and put it in a candle to burn at home."

Three other ladies browsed the shelves of the small store. One side showcased all of Steepe Co.'s teas, the other tea ware. In the middle were all the specials, including a table advertising the newly arrived Golden Monkey tea. Charlotte gasped at the high price. One crate of the tea they'd taken from the docks was worth only a fraction of a bag of Golden Monkey.

Charlotte drifted over to the shelves of teas, not knowing where to start or what she should buy to try. Off to their right was a small attached café. The whole place gave the impression of being an old pub that had been repurposed into a tea shop.

By the time she got to the fourth tea she didn't know, she wished Martin was there to guide her. She brushed her hand over the notebooks in her pockets. She hadn't given Martin his back yet, and may have read most of his notes including all the business ones she didn't understand. Her curiosity had been too great to resist. There'd been no grand secrets, simply mundane reminders and day-to-day notes interspersed with tidbits about tea.

She pulled his notebook and opened it. She flipped through the pages until she landed on the vanilla black tea. Smooth with light notes of vanilla. Decadent with cream. As she read the words she heard them in his voice and that made giddiness pool in her stomach. She grabbed a small bag of the vanilla tea off the shelf.

Mary leaned in close, two bags of tea already in her hands. "What did you find?"

"A vanilla black tea. I think it would be nice to have after dinner."

"Or with scones." Mary glanced over Charlotte's shoulder. "This may sound odd, but I think we are being followed."

"By who?" Charlotte glanced around the shop, but no one looked their way.

"There is a man leaning against the building outside. He did the same while we were dress shopping. I don't think it's a coincidence."

Charlotte turned, but the man had his back to them. He slouched against the shop beside the window, his hat pulled down low. "Who is he?"

"I don't know. Do you think he could be a detective?" Mary grinned. "Oh how exciting! Do you think this has to do with our going to the docks? He must be the man Margaret caught. I should give him a stern talking to about spying on ladies at night." Mary practically vibrated with excitement.

Charlotte glanced back toward the man, unease causing sweat to prickle on the back of her neck. Too many possibilities churned in her mind, each more threatening than the last. He could be following them for the stolen tea. Or maybe someone thought they were responsible for the explosion. Or maybe the man was simply a criminal hoping to kidnap her and ransom her to the Steepe's. Was that what happened to Martin's last fiancée? It would explain all the secrecy surrounding why the engagement fell through. Her sweating hands turned ice cold. "I don't care who he is. I'm not going to let him keep following us. Only someone with bad intentions would resort to stalking us all over."

"I don't see how we can leave without him noticing."

"We need to find another way." Charlotte glanced back down at the notebook. She flipped through until she found the right page, giving it a once over before pocketing the notebook. She started for the counter. The shopkeeper smiled at them. "Good afternoon, ladies. Is there anything I can help you with?" A light accent laced his words, hinting that he'd been born in India instead of Britain. If he was the same shopkeeper mentioned in Martin's notebook, the man made the best chai Martin had ever tasted. His page on that had included a "hire him" in all caps at the bottom.

"Hello, I would like to buy this tea." At least it would finally assuage the guilt over taking the bag from the docks.

"Very good, miss. Is there anything else I can help you find?"

"Are you Arjun?" she asked.

"Yes."

"Arjun, does the shop have a back door?" she asked as she handed over her coins.

His smile fell. "Customers are not allowed in the back, miss."

"She's not just any customer," Mary piped up. "She's Mr. Martin Steepe's fiancée."

He gave them both a dubious look. "I did hear of his new engagement ..." Uncertainty rang cloud and clear in his voice.

"We simply want to leave through the back door is all. There is a man outside who is waiting to harass us when we leave. I'll be sure to let Mr. Steepe know how helpful you were."

The man's uncertainty melted away. He stepped back and opened the door, leading into the back room for them. "The door is straight through at the very back. It comes out in the alleyway."

"Thank you. Next time I hope to try that chai of yours Martin is so fond of."

His smile returned. "Of course, miss."

Crates of tea and tea ware crowded the back room leaving a narrow and short path through the small space. The scent of tea and spices disappeared when she opened the back door as the sour reek of garbage washed over them. Charlotte clapped a hand over her mouth to hold in her squeal. She closed the door behind them, keeping one hand over her nose to guard against the smell.

"This way!" Mary ran down the alley. Charlotte hurried to catch up. It only took a few minutes for them to reach Hyde Park, other ladies shooting them dirty looks as they ran by. They passed the construction underway for The Great Exhibition. Men worked at raising large glass panels into place on the building while others finished removing a tree, roots and all. The size of the space reserved for the Crystal Palace being put up was dizzying.

Mary didn't stop until she reached the lake where swan peddle boats glided across the water. The owner yelled and waved his hands wildly as two young men used magic to race the boats across the pond faster than anyone could peddle them. A woman screamed as if she expected to drown when one of the racers veered close enough for the small wake to gently rock her boat.

Mary's eyes lit up, and Charlotte knew what that must mean before Mary spoke.

"Let's get on a boat." Mary grabbed her hand and rushed to the tiny dock. Charlotte glanced behind them, seeing no sign of the odd man from outside of the tea shop.

A couple climbed out of a boat and as soon as they'd gone, Mary lurched toward it. "I've always wanted to take one of these boats out with a beau," she sighed. "It always seemed so romantic. You should bring yours sometime."

She couldn't imagine Bertram getting into a swan boat to interfere like he loved to do. But a few minutes on the water together with Martin could be exciting. He might actually kiss her then. She felt lightheaded trying to picture it. "I will. And what about you? Who would you bring?"

Mary reached over the side of the boat to skim her fingertips over the water. "I don't know. In truth the idea of revealing my writing to a man is a little daunting."

"Why? You love excitement. If I were you I'd be proud of how popular my writing is."

"I am and I love excitement when no one knows who I am. But I prefer my writing to be private. It feels more freeing that way and I don't worry about what everyone thinks. When I'm Mary Hawke I can be the proper lady everyone expects without drawing too much attention to myself. And then I can go home and write or put on a costume and enjoy excitement on my own terms." She pulled her hand back into the boat. "This little lake was my inspiration for the lake at Hallow Manor. Margaret and I have spent far too much time in these boats."

"My father used to row my Mother and I around in the rowboats when I was a child." Laoise had gone with them once or twice when her mother had been too busy working to come along. And of course she'd fallen in once trying to reach for a duck. Laoise never let fear stop her, and Charlotte had always admired that.

Mary stopped pedaling. Charlotte followed her gaze to the man leaning against a tree. The same man from before, it had to be. The stance and clothing were all the same, except this time his head was angled toward the lake. He clutched a closed newspaper in one hand.

"How did he find us?" Charlotte turned the boat away from him.

"He must be a detective to be this good."

Charlotte aimed the boat for the far side of the lake. "Let's sneak out on the other side."

"And then go where? My father isn't home, and I don't want to lead him to Margaret." Mary peeked out the side of the boat. "Oh no." Her tone sounded more excited than worried.

"What is it?"

"He is walking around the lake."

Sure enough the man meandered along the edge of the lake. Charlotte peddled faster, but it was no use. The man quickened his pace to keep up with them.

"It's not working." Mary stopped peddling to catch her breath.

Charlotte stopped, debating their options. The line for the boats had grown. "We'll go to the bakery. My father can confront whoever the man is. Steer us toward the dock. I'm going to create a distraction." She reached for the swan's head and began tracing the rune spell her father had warned her about. Changing the order of the last two runes changed the spell. After a few mishaps with the runes, her grandfather had carved the pattern into the oven to prevent any others from happening. Her father had told her the story countless times as a warning to always follow the guide on the oven.

"What are you doing?" Mary asked, voice shrill when smoke drifted up from the runes.

Charlotte didn't stop. On the last rune the swan's head burst into flames and Mary screamed.

"Sorry! I don't remember it creating that much fire."

Mary peddled faster. "Why did you have to pick such a hot distraction?" Sweat beaded on both their brows.

"It's one of the only two spells I know."

Everyone waiting in line for a boat shuffled back, gaping as their burning swan pulled up to the dock. The man following them traced his steps back toward the boat rental.

"Are all your boats fiery death traps?" A woman overdressed for the park shrilly demanded as the man running the rentals filled a bucket with lake water. He ignored the woman. The man didn't wait for Charlotte and Mary to get out of the boat. He tossed the bucket of water onto the swan's head. Mary squealed as water splashed onto her. They rushed from the boat as the spell reignited, fresh smoke pouring from the swan.

"What did you do?" The man demanded as he refilled the bucket.

"Sorry," Charlotte said. "I guess it's too hot today."

All at once the women waiting beneath the shade of the nearby trees opened their sun parasols. One woman held hers straight out as she opened it, the parasol knocking into the mysterious man standing at the edge of the water, his gaze pinned on Charlotte. The bump took him by surprise. He struggled to regain his balance, one foot sliding forward in the mud of the shore.

His foot didn't stop sliding. He fell forward, landing with a large splash that hit the woman still loudly complaining about the fiery death traps on the lake. She froze, her mouth wide open. Then she turned and whacked the man with her parasol as he tried to climb out of the lake. The whack pushed him back in onto his behind, splashing her a second time.

"How dare you!" the woman shrieked.

"Go!" Charlotte ran as fast as her legs would move, Mary close behind. A stitch in her side started by the time they made it out of the park. They slowed to a fast walk as they headed in the direction of the bakery. Once they reached Charlotte's favorite book shop, she stopped to catch her breath. "Is he still following us?" She sucked in a large breath before glancing behind them just as the man turned the corner onto their street.

Mary groaned. "He doesn't give up easily, does he?"

"We need to keep going." Charlotte continued on, her attention locked onto the bakery's awning down the road. She held onto Mary's arm, afraid the man would grab either of them at any minute. A few steps away from the bakery relief surged through her. Then Martin stepped outside with a cinnamon bun in one hand.

Charlotte stopped, Mary running into her back.

"Charlotte!" Martin beamed at her. "And Miss Falcon."

"Hawke," Mary corrected in a squeaky voice.

His smile fell. "My apologies. The birds look so alike to me I often mix them up."

"I supposed they do." Her brow furrowed in confusion as she considered his words.

Charlotte glanced over her shoulder, her heart skipping a beat when she saw how close the man was. Only a storefront away. The man grabbed a fresh newspaper from a young boy and held it up, pretending to read. "Martin, can you help us? That man in the brown suit with the newspaper is following us. I don't think he has good intentions."

Martin leaned around them. "That can't be. Roger is the Steepe Company's private detective." He waved. "Roger! How do you do today?"

The man's shoulders slouched as he tucked the newspaper under one arm and slunk up to them.

"Your detective?" Charlotte asked, aghast.

"Yes. I take it your investigation of the explosion at the docks isn't going well." Martin looked down at the water dripping from Roger's coat. "It looks like you fell in the harbor." He waved a hand in the air. "But I don't want to keep you. I'm sure you have plenty of work to do today." His smile returned as he turned his attention to Charlotte. "May I buy you ladies a treat? This is my favorite bakery."

Charlotte started to object, but when she turned to point at Roger she found him already rushing away.

"The couple who run this bakery are lovely," Martin continued as he opened the door for them.

Unable to come up with an excuse to avoid the bakery, Charlotte shuffled in behind Mary. Her mother looked up from the ledger book and smiled. Charlotte held a finger up to her mouth.

"Mr. Steepe, welcome back."

"Thank you. Charlotte, please, let me treat you and Miss Hawke. Anything you'd like."

Behind him her mother held her hands out to the side, as if to ask why she was there. Mary pointed at Charlotte and then her mother, tilting her head to the side. As soon as Martin turned back around she nodded at Mary.

"Everything looks delicious," Mary offered with a strained smile. "Should we get something?"

Charlotte's mother nodded with enthusiasm. "We have fresh beignets."

Her mother knew how to tempt Charlotte. The fried pastry dough was one of Charlotte's favorites. Her mouth watered. "Yes, please."

"Me too," Mary said.

Charlotte's mother handed over the beignets, raising an eyebrow at Charlotte. The corner of her mouth twitched. "Are you two courting?"

Charlotte ran a finger over her neck, but her mother didn't stop.

"We are engaged." Martin smiled as he stepped closer to Charlotte.

"What a lovely couple," Charlotte's mother said as she handed over the beignets. "Please come back again."

Charlotte glared at her mother before heading for the door.

"Such a nice lady," Martin murmured as they left. He checked his pocket watch. "I wish I could stay and chat with you ladies, but I must be on my way. I have a meeting in under an hour about The Great Exhibition. Any chance you are free for afternoon tea tomorrow, Charlotte?"

"That sounds lovely." She pressed her hand against his notebook in her pocket. She'd keep it a day longer and give it back to him tomorrow. By then she will have finished reading all his notes.

As Martin bid them good day and climbed into his carriage, Charlotte noted Roger was nowhere to be seen.

"Bertram must have sent Roger," she said as soon as Martin's carriage pulled away. Martin hadn't, which left Bertram. "If he is going to play dirty to break up my courtship, I'll return his rudeness in kind."

"But what are you going to do about the party? If Mr. Steepe shows up to escort you, he'll find out about the bakery."

That was a good point. One Charlotte hadn't thought of. "Are you going to the party by any chance?"

"As a matter of fact Margaret and I are both going with Father. Want us to pick you up?"

"If you would be so kind, yes. I will make up some excuse for it at tea tomorrow."

Mary glanced up and down the road. "A shame Roger didn't stay. I would have liked to get his business card. The investigator my father currently employs has had no luck tracking down my uncle. I suppose I can ask at the party."

Charlotte turned, jumping when she found her mother standing at the bakery's window, staring out at them, arms crossed over her chest. She sighed. "I suppose I should go explain to my mother. Do you want to come in and try this tea with me?" She held up the bag of vanilla tea.

Mary grinned. "I'd love to."

Chapter 13

C arriages overflowed the drive leading to the stately manor. Charlotte fidgeted, her nerves picking up now that she could see the line of fashionable dresses heading inside. Mary's father stared out the far carriage window, gaze distant. He'd been like that since Charlotte climbed into the carriage. She was certain he hadn't even noticed her.

"Father." Mary shook his arm. "We're here. Please try to look less ..." Mary waved a hand. "Just smile more." She reached over and fixed the buttons on his coat. "And don't forget to speak to Mr. Roquefort about him investing in the company."

He didn't speak until they made it inside. "Mary, look after Margaret."

"We're not children anymore. Mary doesn't need to look after me."

Their father paid the protest no mind as his wandering gaze roved the room.

"Elizabeth," Margaret hissed behind them. She stomped off toward Elizabeth, who tilted her nose in the air when she saw Margaret coming her way.

"I'll never understand those two," Mary said. "I swear they enjoy their rivalry. Margaret gets bored if Elizabeth isn't around to pester at parties."

They slunk against the wall of the large ballroom, soft music playing under the din of conversation. The smell of lilac perfumed the air. The doors at the end were open, guests spilling out into the gardens beyond. Charlotte didn't recognize any of the faces mingling nearby. "Do you know these people?"

Mary took in everyone, taking her time. "I know at least half of them through my father's business connections. Hawke's serials are rather popular, and we have quite a few writers, including a few well-to-do ones who don't want the stigma of writing penny bloods, and so they publish under pen names. They hide behind their silver-fork novels." She lowered her voice. "And most don't know about how extensive our business troubles are. Not yet."

"I won't say a word," Charlotte promised. They drifted to the side of the room, a line of paintings staring down at them. Literally. The magical enchantments brought the paintings to life. In one a sea monster attacked a ship at sea. In another fog drifted through a forest.

"Do you like the enchantments?" Mary asked.

"They make the paintings more interesting if not over the top."

"They do," Mary said as she stared up at the ship. "It's just the sort of magic the wealthy love. It's always about looks and impressing. My father used to have a painting of foolish Icarus falling to his doom when he flew too close to the sun and it gave Margaret nightmares. He wound up selling it for a nice sum that he invested into the business."

Charlotte turned her back to the paintings. "What etiquette should I be aware of? I've never been to a party this large." Charlotte smoothed a wrinkle in her skirt.

"Since a magician is hosting, there will be plenty of guests ignoring the etiquette the nobles hold dear. Magicians seem to derive pleasure from shocking the nobility. You can talk to and dance with anyone you want. No need to worry about formal titles. I'd also suggest expecting the unexpected.

"Last time I was at a party here, a man tried to steal a kiss from one of the Roquefort sisters. She knocked him off a balcony and used magic to leave him dangling there by his right foot. His friends had to help him down." Her expression turned thoughtful. "Has Mr. Steepe mentioned anything about Hawke House?"

"No. He told me he isn't familiar with the company." They spent her last visit sampling more of his teas while he gave her a more in-depth tour of the Steepe garden and house. She'd been too caught up in listening to him narrate the tour and the tea to think to push the Hawke issue.

"No matter. Father said he has an interested investor. Maybe Roquefort will invest so father doesn't have to sell." Her lips pressed together as she watched the men. "Oh, there is Mr. Steepe. Well I'm off to go drink far too much champagne." Mary grabbed a flute off a maid's tray. "None of this would have happened if father had agreed to let me keep an eye on Uncle," Mary grumbled under her breath as she headed toward the other side of the room.

Charlotte didn't have long to agonize over Mary's predicament or her own writing languishing in her drawer. The sight of Martin dressed in a fashionable, tailored suit sent her mind veering off track. He spotted her and a smile lit up his face as he set off in her direction.

"Charlotte." He gave her his stiff, formal bow. His brow creased as the utmost look of seriousness replaced his smile. "I'm glad you came. You look beautiful, as always."

She smiled back. "Good evening. I've been meaning to return this to you." She held out his little notebook. "I'm sorry I kept it so long." She'd already read it enough times to memorize all his tea notes.

He pocketed the notebook. "Thank you for returning it. I was looking for it this morning at my meeting. I've received official permission to serve hot tea at The Great Exhibition! With people coming from all over the world it is going to be quite the opportunity to get my tea in the hands of more buyers and expand the business."

"That sounds wonderful. I can't imagine anyone else selling tea as good as yours."

"Would you come with me on opening day to see the shop and the other displays? I would love to have your company."

The butterflies in her stomach did somersaults. "I would love to." A chance to see The Great Exhibition before the crowds arrived, it would be quite the bragging point. Finally something to talk about at the dull parties her mother dragged her to. But the convincing didn't work on herself. The butterflies swooping at the idea to have another chance to spend time with Martin couldn't be tricked into believing she wasn't going just to see him. Despite his awkward moments, she appreciated his honesty unlike Bertram's false charms.

"Mr. Steepe," a man said as he stepped up beside Martin. "I was hoping to find you here."

"Mr. Stonewall," Martin said. "A pleasure to see you."

The man laughed, clapping Martin on the back. "Still no better at remembering names I see. It's Roquefort. Who's this young lady?" He gave Charlotte a polite smile. Behind him Bertram inched closer and closer.

"This is my fiancée, Miss Charlotte Graham."

Surprise crossed the man's face. "I hadn't heard. Congratulations on your engagement." He gave Charlotte a nod. "I never imagined your plan to make my academic research on magic available to all would be such a wild success. I also heard what you did for Mr. Pemberly's business. I have a friend who would love to consult with you soon if you've got the time. May I introduce you later when he arrives?"

"I would love to meet him. I'm always happy to meet a fellow businessman or magician."

"Great. We'll talk to you later." Roquefort stepped into the crowd, veering toward his next target.

"Do you often do business consultations?" The ladies at the party gave them a wide berth as they went on the prowl for available men. None of them gave Martin more than a quick glance, choosing to focus their attentions on other prospects.

"It is not a service I offer, but I have been asked often this past year. Everyone seems to think I can help the magicians looking to get into business."

"Are you able to help them?"

Martin scrunched his face in thought. "I suppose I do. It tends to come down to a matter of marketing or branding or sometimes location." He frowned. "I've heard some people think I have a gift for business, which is why my father and Bertram are not convinced by the tea shop. They think it is below me and I should be chasing greater ambitions. I plan to use The Great Exhibition to prove to them that tea can be profitable and respectable in its own right. The last thing I want is to go into something like building factories that prey on the poor and children for cheap labor."

"I think your tea shop is wonderful and there is no reason you shouldn't do something you love. I visited your main shop recently and loved it. Mary likes to visit it often as well."

His smile returned. "I'm glad you understand. Talking to you about this is much easier than trying to convince Bertram or my father who are more focused on profits than anything else. I invest elsewhere to please my father, but my investments don't bring me the same satisfaction as my tea."

"Because none of them feel like a warm hug?"

He chuckled. "Exactly." He stared into her eyes, silence passing over them as neither could look away. Finally Martin cleared his voice as a new song began. "Would you have this dance with me?"

"Yes." Her voice came out breathless as she focused on his smile. Something about his attention made her crave more and more of it, and all thoughts of Hawke House and Bertram fled. They headed for the dance floor where a magical mist covering the floor gave the impression the dancers were gliding through clouds. She leaned closer to Martin, wishing he would kiss her no matter who saw. Forget the swan boats. Dancing through clouds with him was far better. His brow furrowed in concentration as they danced.

The dance ended far too soon with fantasies of future parties and dances floating through her mind.

"I believe it is my turn to have a dance next," Bertram said as he sidled up beside her. His charming smile made her cheeks puff in anger.

Martin stepped away, giving Bertram room to take his place. Charlotte opened her mouth to protest, but the music began and Bertram spun her away from Martin as the Viennese Waltz started. She spluttered in indignation.

"What do you think you are doing?" she demanded as she struggled to keep up with the dance.

"What do you think you're doing?" he snapped back. "You were supposed to tell him, and yet here we are. Quit wasting my family's time." The dance gave them plenty of time spent dancing side by side to argue despite the lively steps and skips not matching their heated anger. The couple ahead of them stared into each other's eyes, the perfect example of young love. She'd rather spend her time staring into Martin's eyes than arguing with Bertram.

"Tell him yourself," she taunted, "Or are you afraid at this point he won't care?"

"No. I warned you and you didn't listen. It's time for me to step in and do what needs done to look after my cousin's well-being."

"His well-being? I think you are angry he is the family heir instead of you."

Bertram tightened his grip on Charlotte's waist. "Don't make presumptions you know nothing about." His arm wrapped around her waist as they spun first one way, and then the other.

"I think I understand well enough." He moved with an elegance that made her feel clumsy in comparison, but her anger burned hotter than her embarrassment. "Martin can decide for himself what he wants and you can keep your nose out."

"You've gotten too stubborn. Learn your place." He stepped on her foot and she kneed him in the shin in return. The rest of the dance continued that way, each of them trying to step on the other's foot while they dodged and struggled to stay in step to the song. When the song came to an end Bertram's head swiveled this way and that as he searched for Martin. "Perhaps next time your dancing will be more graceful."

"I could say the same about you."

His lips curled in anger. Then they both spotted Martin. He stood beside a table full of teapots chatting with Roquefort and another man. Roquefort held a teapot up higher for the gathering crowd to see. Martin's gaze strayed to Charlotte before turning back to the host. Bertram hissed something under his breath

Charlotte didn't catch. Then he spun her toward him, keeping an arm around her waist.

"What are you doing?"

"Ending the engagement just like I ended Martin's last one."

Her thoughts tripped over themselves as she absorbed his meaning. "You murdered her, didn't you? You monster. You're as bad as ... as Frankenstein!" She tried to pull away but he held her in place.

"What? No!" His words dripped with offense. "Who do you think I am? She's right over there by the door drinking champagne beside Mrs. Pemberly. And Frankenstein was the doctor, not the monster."

"You would know!" She glanced toward the door. A pretty woman dressed in a teal gown stood beside an older woman, her posture rigid and her face sullen. When Charlotte turned back Bertram leaned in closer. Too close. She froze, unwilling to believe he was about to do what she thought he was about to do.

But then he did, his eyes still on Martin as his lips flopped against hers like a fish. A woman near them loudly gasped, her reaction drawing more attention as the dancers around them gawked. A few halted and others joined. They all watched, sending Charlotte's heart pattering in terror. She thought she caught sight of Mary nearby on the dance floor with a man dressed in all black.

Then Charlotte slapped Bertram. He tried to dodge, causing her to whack him in the nose instead of the cheek. His look of shock sent satisfaction slithering through her. "How dare you? I'm engaged to your cousin and have no interest in anyone else," she said, her voice loud enough for those around her to hear. She lifted a hand to her forehead. "Someone please get this rake away from me." A man behind them snickered and red blazed across Bertram's cheeks. A dribble of red started from his left nostril, picking up speed as the flow grew heavier. He fumbled for his handkerchief, cursing.

"He's bleeding!" a woman shouted.

"Are you all right, miss?" the man to her left asked.

Charlotte gave him the saddest expression she could muster. "Could you escort me off the dance floor please?"

"Of course, of course." He stepped away from his dance partner with a quick apology, but the woman was too busy reaching for the woman next to her. They pressed their heads together and began furiously whispering, stealing glances at Charlotte. She kept her head high, refusing to let Bertram embarrass her.

Martin was caught up in the host's frantic gesturing. She stepped closer, guessing Martin hadn't seen a thing. Relief surged through her. At least this way she could give him her side first. Set Bertram up as the villain he was.

"This is utterly marvelous!" the host gushed as he inspected his cup of tea. "Please tell me you will plan to show this at The Great Exhibition next week?"

"Yes. I've perfected it as much as I can. I plan to open up orders for it there."

Questions flew from the crowd. Martin held up a hand to quiet them. "Visit my booth at The Great Exhibition to learn more about all my enchanted offerings. You can also visit my tea shop anytime."

"... and then a bird flew from the sky, casting a large shadow across the ground as it dove. The warriors scattered, leaving only one willing to face the creature." The droning voice was quieter than the others, the story making no sense to Charlotte. Then she spotted the teapot in the center of the table. Steam curled from the spout, moving as if it were a mouth. No one paid the story much mind, too engrossed in their host's ravings.

A talking teapot. If not for Bertram's kiss, she would have considered it the biggest surprise of the evening.

"You have the most interesting ways of using magic," Roquefort said as he clapped Martin on the back.

She made her way to Martin's side, unsure of how she would explain to him.

Another man stepped up to the magician, pulling his attention away from Martin.

"Is it true you have a new trick you're unveiling at the Great Exhibition?"

The magician grinned, seemingly pleased at the question.

Martin jumped when her fingers brushed his arm.

"Sorry to interrupt, but I need to speak to you." She widened her eyes, hoping dramatics would work in her favor. "Something dreadful has happened."

Martin stiffened. "Is everything all right?"

"Can we go somewhere more private?" she shifted as the crowd around her closed in.

"This way." Martin led her out of the ballroom, the music instantly disappearing as she stepped through the doorway, a thin veil of magic ghosting over her. Guests eager to escape somewhere quieter crowded the hallway and parlor one door down. Martin mumbled the name of each room as he passed the doors. "Here we are."

He ushered her into a room empty of guests. Paintings covered the walls with chairs situated in the middle of the floor. An enchantment on the floor gave the appearance of water with a path of stepping stones leading through the gallery.

"Are all of his rooms this enchanted?"

"He likes to impress. It's why he enjoys performing on stage. He bought this manor from a bankrupt nobleman a decade ago and has been filling it with enchantments ever since. Personally I prefer utility over entertainment. I also find it strange how the magicians speak against the nobility, but imitate their lavish lifestyles as much as possible."

She stepped onto the first stepping stone behind him, pausing to poke at the floor with her toe. The water rippled, but she could feel the floor whole and solid. "Wasn't your last fiancée from nobility?" Asking made her feel small. Her new dress and the enchanted surroundings all made her feel like an impostor. She belonged in the bakery kitchen, not in this enchanted art gallery. If a noble fiancée couldn't survive Bertram's meddling, how could she?

Martin clasped her hand in his, tugging her out of her thoughts. "My father chose her, not me. It is why I fought to choose my next fiancée myself. I wanted to find someone I was better suited with."

Charlotte found her own insecurity reflected in his gaze.

"You are much kinder to me than she was. She found my interest in tea and my lacking social manners embarrassing. No matter how hard I tried, I always felt unable to please her."

"Women can be fickle. That is why I prefer the hunt," the man in the painting to Martin's left said. He stood with one foot atop a boar's carcass, a rifle leaning against one shoulder.

"I've never enjoyed hunting."

The man in the painting stepped off the boar. "Not one for hunting? I say! If I could leave this painting I would give you a right thrashing, sir."

Martin turned away from the painting. "Shall we continue on?" They stepped deeper into the gallery, pausing in a section full of landscapes where no paintings could eavesdrop. Beautiful as they were, she couldn't focus on the paintings. Her attention kept wandering back to Martin.

Charlotte sucked in a breath. "Bertram kissed me after we danced."

Martin froze, his gaze locked onto the seashore in front of him.

"I slapped him and quite a few other dancers saw. I want to be clear I have no interest in him. He mentioned he was the reason your last engagement ended. I understand if you don't want to talk about it, but I'd like to know what happened."

Martin sighed, his shoulders lifting. "She decided she was more interested in Bertram. He turned her down, but not before I found them kissing in my parlor."

"I'm sorry, but he kissed me in front of everyone in the ballroom." She studied him, wondering how hard she should push. "Are you sure he isn't trying to ruin our engagement on purpose?" She reached for his coat, bunching the fabric in her hand. "I'm afraid he'll succeed in that, and I wouldn't be able to bear it." Her voice trembled.

Martin's expression hardened. "I'll talk to him."

"If only I could forget his kiss." Charlotte shifted closer, angling her face up toward Martin.

"He shouldn't have kissed you."

"Maybe you could help me think of something else," Charlotte tried again, pushing her arm against his.

"Well, there are plenty of beautiful paintings in here." He held out a hand, gesturing toward the landscape beside them.

She pressed her lips together, in frustration, seeing no choice but to be direct with him. "I'm trying to get you to kiss me."

He turned to her, his mouth parted slightly in surprise. His eyebrows shot up. "Kiss you?"

She nodded.

His gaze lowered to her lips. After spending a moment in thought he leaned down. He paused halfway, their gazes connecting. Charlotte's stomach tightened. She held her breath in anticipation.

Then he dipped her. Her breath whooshed from her in surprise as she held onto his shoulders. He pressed his lips to hers. His citrus cologne was a welcomed scent after Bertram's muskier scent. Martin's soft lips moved in time with hers, the opposite of Bertram's distracted kiss. One of the paintings whistled at them and Martin pulled away.

He straightened his cravat. "Was the dip too much?"

"Not at all." She lifted a hand to her lips and considered pulling him back into a second kiss.

"Mr. Steepe! How fortuitous." A middle-aged man stepped into the room. A younger man with spectacles that made Charlotte think of a secretary followed close behind. "I'd like to ask you for some advice on the location of my new storefront. I have two options in mind and would love to hear your thoughts."

"You're a rather popular man tonight, aren't you?" Charlotte whispered.

"Your attentions are the only ones I care about," Martin said with somber conviction that made her giggle. Only he could make such a romantic statement sound overly serious.

"I don't mind your popularity as long as you promise me another dance soon."

"As many as you want."

Chapter 14

"Are you leaving soon?" Charlotte asked Mary.

"Hmmm?" Mary asked, attempting to drink from her glass, too distracted to notice it was already empty.

Charlotte followed her attention to the dance floor, but Mary's attention never lingered anywhere in particular for long.

"Who or what are you looking for?"

"A man dressed in all black. He disappeared on me when Bertram's nose started bleeding. He looks like Lord Hallow. Too much like Lord Hallow. I have no idea who he is, and I want to find out."

"I didn't notice." But she'd noticed the way Martin tilted his head whenever someone started speaking to him. The way his brow creased in concentration before he responded. And his soft lips! She wanted to kiss him again and again. "Do you plan to leave soon?"

"It's only midnight. The party has hours to go yet." Mary stood on her tiptoes to search the crowd around them.

"I'm usually in bed by now preparing to wake up in about five hours for the bakery." The thrill of the night was fading as fatigue crept in.

"I can't leave yet. Not until I find out who this Lord Hallow man is. It is uncanny how similar they are." Mary wandered off again, her head swiveling this way and that. Charlotte waited a minute, but once it became clear Mary wasn't coming back she sighed and went in search of Martin. She found him in a circle of businessmen near the door. When he noticed her he excused himself from the group.

"Can your coachman take me home? I can't stay awake much longer. I'm accustomed to early nights and early mornings."

"Early mornings do make for productive days." He nodded as he spoke. "Please allow me to escort you home."

"That isn't necessary." Her tired mind grasped at any excuse she could think of. "I'd hate to make you cut your time short on my account."

"Nonsense. I prefer early mornings too. When I wake up at noon it feels as though I've wasted half the day. I'll have the carriage fetched immediately."

She relented, unable to find the energy to argue or imagine waking up at noon. She felt like she'd wasted too much of the day on the rare occasions she slept until nine.

He gathered his box of teapots and walked her outside. The stars shone in the cloudless sky, the full moon lighting up the night bright enough the little magical orbs lining the stairs weren't needed.

"It feels too quiet out here." She didn't realize the thought had slipped out until Martin replied.

"The night always feels melancholy to me after a great day. I don't like knowing it's all about to end. I prefer mornings because I like having the whole day ahead of me to enjoy."

"That is an apt way of putting it. I agree." Part of her wanted to go back inside and dance the night away, but the siren call of sleep was too strong and the ride ahead of them would be long enough to make resisting sleep all the more difficult. "Thank you for inviting me. I'm glad I got to dance with you."

"I am too. I hope I didn't step on your feet. I was a late learner."

"Not once." She gave him a sly smile. "The kiss was also nice."

He brushed his hand over hers. "I thought so too. We'll have to do both again."

She pressed a hand over her mouth to hold in her giggle at the sincerity in his voice as though both kissing and dancing were things to put on his schedule.

The carriage rolled up, and the coachman jumped down to take the box from Martin and shoved it inside. Martin waved the coachman off and offered her a hand to help her into the carriage.

"What is your favorite place to visit?"

"My favorite?" she asked as she climbed inside.

"For next time. Let me take you somewhere you love. I want to learn more about what you like."

No man had ever asked her before. It made her want to kiss him again, but in the darkness of the carriage she couldn't see well enough. Her lips might miss their mark. "My favorite place is Brook's Bookstore. I like to browse and then have a light meal at the cafe down the road."

"Then next time I will take you to the bookstore and the cafe."

"I look forward to it." She slid the curtain open, letting the moonlight fill the carriage as they headed back to the city. She turned, catching the play of moonlight over Martin's profile. It was as if he grew more handsome every time she saw him. He may not be as impressive as his cousin, but there was an understated elegance to him. "What's your favorite place?"

"My tea shop followed by home. I'm afraid I'm a man of simple pleasures."

"That suits you." She pictured him reading in his study with a cup of tea in hand and Oolong at his feet. The image filled her with longing to be seated next to him, writing or reading, but she didn't dare place herself there. Not yet. "Did you ever love her?" She twisted a fistful of her skirt.

"Who?"

"Your last fiancée. Did you ever love her?"

"The engagement only lasted three months. She was ..." He shifted in his seat. "She was more of a coffee drinker," he said, emphasizing coffee with distaste. He said no more, as if that was enough to explain everything.

"Oh." Those words coming from anyone else would have left her baffled, but his passion for tea was enough for her to understand his distaste. She didn't need the small details. They wouldn't matter anyway if he truly wanted to marry someone of noble birth instead of a baker's daughter. But they'd kissed. Maybe her mother would be right. If he fell enough for her, her station might not matter. She clung to that hope.

The carriage halted without warning, sending her sprawling forward against Martin. "What is going on?" She took her time righting herself, savoring the warmth of him. He helped her up, murmuring apologies as if the halt were his fault.

"Mr. Steepe?" the coachman called out, his voice wavering.

The carriage door opened, revealing a figure silhouetted by the moonlight, the dark forest yawning behind him. A mask covered the top half of the man's face beneath a hat pulled low. A cloak hid part of his suit, but not enough. The suit and strong jaw gave him away and Charlotte groaned. Would he ever give up?

Martin gasped. "I know who you are. I can't believe it!" He smacked a hand against his thigh.

Finally, thought Charlotte. Now there would be proof his cousin couldn't be trusted.

"Is that so?" the highwayman rumbled, his voice mocking. He pulled a pistol from beneath his cloak. "Then I hope I won't need this."

Charlotte's heart stuttered. Surely Bertram wouldn't turn the gun on own cousin? Or her?

"You're Dick Turpin!"

Charlotte and the intruder both gaped at Martin.

"That is clearly Bert—" Charlotte started.

"That's right," Bertram said, quick to interrupt with each word louder than the last, making him sound more confused than confident. "I'm Dick Turpin." He puffed out his chest and posed with one hand on his hip and the pistol aimed at the sky. "And no one else."

"I can't believe it! This is the man who robbed your parents." Martin looked to Charlotte for confirmation. Her mind struggled to make sense of how Martin's mind worked or the connection to Dick Turpin, already having forgotten her earlier lie at the family dinner.

"Yes, I, Dick Turpin, have robbed plenty of people."

"Including my parents" Charlotte said, settling her steely gaze on the highwayman and daring him to contradict her.

His mouth puckered. "Did I? How would you know I was the one who robbed them if you weren't there?"

"Because you match the description. My mother said it was an exceptionally ugly man who took her purse."

"I'm wearing a mask!"

"Ugly on the inside," she spat out.

The highwayman punched the side of the carriage.

Martin reached for Charlotte's hands. "I'm sorry about your parents."

"I don't think that's what's important at the moment." She glared at the highwayman. "It's a little odd isn't it? Seeing a highwayman here?"

"I go wherever I please whenever I want." He turned to Martin. "I believe you have something valuable and I want it. Stand and ... and deliver!"

Martin pulled his hand from Charlotte's as he started to stand. "I don't have any money on me."

"No, not money. And don't stand. I didn't mean it that way. I meant hand over your valuables. Sit back down." The highwayman shoved Martin down by the shoulder. "You have an enchanted object I heard much raving about tonight. I want it."

"You're stopping us over teaware?" Charlotte raised her voice. "Are you serious?"

"The future of his business is worth stopping over." He waved the gun at the box beneath the seat. "Pull it out."

Martin did, his movements slow as he cradled the box and pulled it onto his lap. "If you wanted one you could have simply asked. You can even order one at The Great Exhibition come May."

"Shut up and open it."

Martin's expression turned sour. "And to think everyone thinks my manners are terrible." He opened the box, revealing the teapot inside.

The highwayman scowled. "What is that?"

"It's a Gongfu Cha set from China." Muffled Chinese came from the teapot. "Sorry, wrong lid." Martin switched out the lid just as the highwayman yanked it from him, black gloves hiding his hands.

"I am the teapot of Lu Yu, the author of The Classic of Tea. The book includes a wealth of information on tea—"

"I don't need the details!"

"'I don't need the details,' the highwayman cried, his voice rife with impatience,'" the teapot said.

The skin showing beneath the mask reddened. "Is this a joke?"

"The teapot is recording this encounter for future stories. It's what Louie does. Although usually he doesn't do it aloud. He must not like you."

"Louie?" The highwayman's hand clenched on his pistol.

"I very well can't call him Lu Yu. That was the maker, not the tea pot."

The teapot continued his recording aloud. "'Is this a joke?' the highwayman asked, his face coloring in embarrassment over what a fool he was."

"Enough!" The highwayman shoved the teapot back onto Martin's lap. "Where is the other enchanted object? I refuse to believe this one is worth anything."

"I am priceless to those who understand my worth," the teapot declared.

Martin slapped his forehead. "My prototype! I knew I was forgetting something! I left it behind. That's what I get for not making a checklist in my notebook."

"You forgetful blunderbuss!" The highwayman slapped the side of the carriage a second time.

"Do you want my earrings?" Charlotte offered, hoping it'd get him to go away.

"But don't you dare lay a hand on the lady," Martin added

The highwayman made a noise of disgust. "I have no interest in touching the lady. Keep your gaudy jewelry."

She scoffed in offense. "How dare you!" She reached down and pulled off her shoe and chucked it at his head, the heel hitting his left eyebrow.

He hissed and slapped a hand over his left eye. She reached for her other shoe and he staggered away from the carriage. Lanterns bobbed through the trees around the bend, alerting them to another carriage coming. The highwayman took off into the darkness, stumbling over a large fallen branch.

"That's right, run you coward!" Charlotte roared.

The other carriage continued on past them without stopping. Drunken laughter drifted from inside.

Martin hopped out and fetched Charlotte's shoe. When he returned with it he wore the look of utmost seriousness as he slid it back onto her foot. "You were very brave. Thank you for doing what I couldn't. Next time I will better protect your honour."

"Next time? I hope I never get stopped by a highwayman again."

"M-Mr. Steepe?" The coachman called out.

"We're fine. Let's get Miss Graham home first."

"Erm, I don't know where she lives."

Charlotte gave him her road. "Stop right on the corner near the row of azaleas." She'd pretend to go around back of the house then sneak down the road to the bakery.

Martin went back to his seat, and they got back on their way. She reached for her necklace, her sour mood deepening as she mulled over the highwayman's words. "Do you think my jewelry is gaudy?"

He glanced down at her necklace. "I don't know a thing about jewelry, but I think it looks pretty on you."

Honest to a fault, she thought. "Are you sure you didn't recognize the highwayman?"

"Something about him did seem rather familiar."

"Did he remind you of Bertram at all?"

"Perhaps a bit." He rubbed his chin. "But Bertram is no highwayman. With his business endeavors, he has no need to resort to such lowly tactics." He rested against the side of the carriage. "Although it's beginning to feel like I know him less and less. I never would have suspected he had any interest in kissing you."

"I don't think he has a true interest in me, nor do I have any desire for him to ever kiss me again. Please make sure he doesn't."

"I will talk to him as soon as I can." The carriage left the forest and his gaze turned to the moon. "Everything was easier when we were boys. With a house full of younger sisters to look after and his father having passed, Bertram was determined to have his own successful business. He's had success anyone would be proud of, but I worry he still doesn't think it is enough. Not since he's gotten it in his head to try for a title. Now he is obsessed with our family's reputation and mingling with nobility. He thinks it will help land his sisters good husbands and help the family's fortunes, but I wish he'd think more about himself instead. There is far more to life than money. Being sick taught me to appreciate the small pleasures."

Why did he have to love his cousin so much? His devotion made her want to hug Martin and strangle Bertram all at once. Martin didn't deserve whatever Bertram was up to. "What do you want outside of your business?"

He clasped her hand in his. "I already found what I want."

Her heart beat wildly. His sincere tone set her on fire.

"Please accept my apologies for everything that went wrong this evening. I hope you at least enjoyed our dancing." The worry in his voice increased the molten fire burning in her core.

She leaned across, aiming for his mouth but catching his chin in the darkness. Embarrassed, she started to pull away, but he stopped her. He pulled her onto the seat beside him. Then with one hand cradling the back of her head, he kissed her, soft and slow, taking his time enjoying her lips. She sank into the kiss, wishing it would never end.

Chapter 15

"I want a tart today," Laoise said as she handed over the latest letter. She pointed at a tart on display. "That one." Charlotte handed over the tart before ripping into the letter. Laoise had become their messenger and Martin being Martin never questioned how his letters reached Charlotte despite the lack of address. The letter confirmed their picnic for that afternoon as long as the nice weather held.

Laoise took a bite of tart before leaning against the counter. "What was it like kissing Bertram?"

"Awful." She narrowed her eyes. "Why are you interested in discussing this again? I thought you didn't like him."

"I don't, but a man that handsome...well a girl can't help but to wonder. I would have let him kiss me too."

"Bertram kisses like a fish."

"A pity that."

"Martin is a much better kisser."

"Ah! So you have kissed him then." Laoise pumped her hand in triumph. "I knew I'd get you to admit to it somehow."

Charlotte sighed. She'd been holding that secret in, savoring it for herself. "I still haven't told him what I am though. He's going to leave me, isn't he?" She rested her head in her hands, leaning her elbows against the counter. "If I didn't love this bakery so much, I'd wish I were someone else. He's so ..." She sighed again.

"Don't get lovesick on me." Laoise shoved the rest of the tart into her mouth to free up her hands. She grabbed Charlotte by the shoulders and shook her. "All the other maids lose their good sense when they sigh over a man like that."

"Are you telling me you haven't sighed over the Steepe's butler? What happened to you trying to seduce him last year?"

"I gave up. I decided he is too boring and strict for my tastes. I'd like a man who enjoys something more exciting than polishing the silver."

"How do you know he doesn't like excitement?"

"Because he is afraid of horses and nags the same way my mother does, and there is nothing less attractive in a man." Laoise reached for the pages laid out on the counter. Charlotte jerked them away and hid them in her apron. "Your book I take it?"

"Yes, and I think I should burn it. No one wants to read about a murderess running a bakery when they've all read and watched Mr. Todd's story."

"That was one of the best plays you've ever dragged me to. What are you going to work on next?"

"I have no idea! I can't stop worrying over Mr. Steepe to concentrate." She regretted giving him his notebook back. She wanted to reread his writing. Study his taste in tea.

"Why don't you get that new writer friend of yours to read it? Or take inspiration from your life and write a romance? Or a baking cookbook? Oh, and two loaves of white sandwich bread. We're low on kitchen staff until next week."

Charlotte wrapped up two of their best loaves. "You're right. Maybe I should ask Mary to give it a read. She'd know better than me if it has any potential." Feedback could help her figure out the direction of her next project. And until then she could work on a recipe to pair with some of her favorite Steepe teas.

"I expect to hear about The Great Exhibition once you go." She grabbed the bread and paid. "I wish I could stay longer but I have other groceries to get. If I don't get back in time the butler will complain and give me an extra chore. I don't know how a man like that can stand to serve Mr. Steepe. They are complete opposites."

Charlotte's mother strolled in with a fresh tray of bread. "Laoise, good morning."

"Good mornin', Mrs. Graham. Please tell Mr. Graham I said hello." She waved as she backed out of the bakery.

Charlotte's mother stepped behind the counter just as a new customer arrived. "You go get ready for your picnic. I can handle this." She paused. "You're still going to the picnic, right?"

"Yes, Mother."

"Good. Try fluttering your eyelashes at him. Tell him he's handsome."

Charlotte groaned. "Please, no more of your advice."

Her mother smiled and turned to greet the customers as the second morning wave trickled in. Charlotte headed upstairs, her worries turning to what to wear. Roquefort's party had gone so well, not including Dick Turpin's appearance, that she wanted to keep up the momentum. Steal another kiss or two. She smiled as she surveyed her dress options, her mind drifting back to the long kisses inside the carriage and the warmth of his hands on her.

She waited for the carriage down her street in front of the house she had herself dropped off by last time. According to Martin's letter he would be meeting her at the park, but she arrived early in case anyone tried knocking on the door. She didn't want to heap more embarrassment upon herself. The wind tugged at her skirts and she pulled her shawl tighter against the spring chill that refused to leave the air.

She buried her nose deeper in the pages in her hand. To think she'd gotten behind on Twilight at Hallow Manor! It was becoming more and more clear Alice felt torn between Lord Hallow and the vampire hunter. She couldn't decide which one to trust.

The carriage pulled up, and the coachman jumped down to open the door for her.

"Thank you," she mumbled as she climbed inside, riveted to the scene of Alice sneaking through the house at night after waking to a scream. She carried nothing but a candle stub to light her way through the pitch black manor. The floor creaked behind her and Alice froze, certain the vampire had come for her at last.

"Hello, Miss Graham."

Charlotte screamed, tossing her papers at the voice. Bertram looked unimpressed and smug all at once as he opened the door and climbed inside. "What are you doing here?" She seethed as she bent over to gather up the pages before Betram could trample them.

"Sharing a ride. My carriage suffered an unfortunate pothole when I left Mr. Roquefort's party and needs repairs."

"Don't tell me you also encountered a certain highwayman. Or perhaps fleeing in the night had consequences for you." She grabbed the last page and snapped the stack of papers.

Bertram widened his eyes in faux innocence. "Why I have no idea of what you are talking about. Are you certain you are feeling all right?"

"Attempting to steal from your cousin is despicable. He deserves better."

Bertram's jaw clenched. "Speaking of my cousin, I finally discovered why you have been feigning interest in him."

"I'm not feigning anything."

"Does that mean you have no interest in Hawke House?" Bertram opened the folder on his lap and removed a contract. "I finalized the papers this morning. I own Hawke now." He handed her a contract.

"You?" Charlotte wrinkled the contract as her hands clenched, shards of ice sinking in her stomach. "Why would you buy Hawke?"

"To give you what you've really been after. Let's make a deal. Tell Martin who you really are and call off the wedding, and Hawke House stays open. Keep lying to my cousin, and they're done for. Your friend Mary can say goodbye to the family business. I prefer Varney the Vampire to that Lord Hallow nonsense anyway."

Charlotte hadn't been a fan of Varney and grew too bored of the character complaining about his vampiric condition. She held her tongue, remembering Mary's pen name wasn't common knowledge. The popularity of her story would surely save her, though she'd have no choice but to switch to a different publishing company. But if the company meant as much to Mary as the bakery did to Charlotte ... Charlotte couldn't live with that guilt. "Is that why you had Roger follow me? To find some blackmail on me?"

He smirked. "I'm rather pleased with the results."

"Will you stop at nothing to break up our engagement?"

"I'll not have my family taken advantage of by a strumpet trying to climb the social ladder."

She snorted. "I don't think you are trying to save him. You want to ruin Martin and become heir in his place."

He clicked his tongue in annoyance. "If I shut down the business, I also hope to buy the Hawkes' house. I could even hire your friend Mary as a maid if she wants to stay."

"You stay away from her. This doesn't involve her." Her hands fisted.

"Oh but it does now. I leave her family's future in your hands."

She folded the contract and slipped it into the pocket she'd sewn into her dress, her mind racing to find a new plan. She couldn't find a way out of this. Not with the contract signed. But that didn't mean she had to roll over and give up. There had to be some way out of this, but her rising panic made it hard to think. Her palms sweat all while Bertram sat looking smug and pleased with himself.

The carriage pulled to a stop, and she rushed out of the door to escape the stifling air.

"Charlotte!" Martin greeted with open arms. He glanced past her. "Bertram, is your carriage not fixed yet?"

"This evening, hopefully" Bertram knocked on the wall. "Let's get going. I don't want to be late."

Martin's smile fell. "Are you sure you don't want to stay for a few minutes? The fresh air will do you some good."

"I don't have time." Bertram shut the door and Martin sighed.

"He never has time for anything but business. I wish he would take more time to relax."

Charlotte couldn't agree. The farther away Bertram was the better. "Have you considered sending him on holiday to the seaside? Or abroad?"

"That is an excellent idea." He disappeared into his thoughts, his gaze distant.

"Martin?"

He blinked, coming back to the present. "Our blanket is set up. Shall we?" He extended his arm and she took it.

Martin had found them a spot beneath a tree. Ahead of them sat Prince Albert's latest accomplishment: The Crystal Palace. The gigantic behemoth of a building was made of glass panels, reminding her of a greenhouse. She couldn't imagine how The Great Exhibition could fill a building that large. She stared at it, shielding her eyes from the sunshine glaring off the glass.

Martin yammered off facts about the building, but Charlotte's attention kept drifting back to the contract in her pocket. After the kiss, she didn't doubt Bertram would make good on his threat. He'd probably cackle as he shut Hawke's doors. He'd savor every minute of it.

"Albert ordered troops to march through to make sure the glass wouldn't shatter," Martin said as Charlotte tried to focus on him.

"Is it safe?" The thought of all that glass raining down was fit for a horror penny blood. Her mind turned that idea over before dismissing it as too gruesome.

"Completely. I've already been inside to set up my little tea shop. I can't wait for you to see it."

"Are you excited for it?"

"Yes, and now I'm excited to have a new audience to showcase my teas to, but there is a lot of pressure. My father is of the mind I should sell off the tea business and focus my energy elsewhere. I want to prove him and Bertram wrong. Prove to them I know what I'm doing and that I don't need to switch to a different business." He rubbed at his stubble. "I felt like my sickness disappointed my father when I was a child. Bertram was more the son he wanted. I've always felt like I've been following in my cousin's footsteps instead of my own path until I opened my tea shop." He opened the picnic basket and pulled out a little tin. He heated up the water with magic and scooped the tea into the pot to steep.

"I don't think you should follow in Bertram's footsteps. You don't need them." The contract pressed against her side, reminding her of how cruel he could be. "I like you best when you are simply Martin." She tilted her head, surveying him. The hair on his chin and upper lip looked as though he hadn't shaved in three days. "Are you growing out a goatee?"

He stroked the hair on his chin. "I didn't mean to. I've been busy setting up my shop in the Crystal Palace the last few days and well …" He shifted, fingers twitching, "I started reading The String of Pearls. I haven't let my valet shave me since."

Charlotte laughed. "What do you think of it?"

"Very exciting. I've never read anything like it before. Oolong has a habit of sneaking up on me while I'm reading it. He makes me jump every time."

"You should check out some of Hawke's serials next. I love sitting down by the fireplace to read all the new chapters when they release. I look forward to it every week."

"I will."

The teapot poured their drinks, and he handed her a cup with silver filigree. He didn't take his attention off her. Realizing he was waiting for her decision on the tea, she took a sip. A hint of vanilla hit her followed by the refreshing tang of orange. "Oh! Delicious. This would pair perfectly with a chocolate treat." The pairing would be heaven.

He reached into the picnic basket and pulled out a small tea tin. He handed it to her.

She read the script across the front. "Charlotte's tea. Did you make this for me?"

"Yes. I hope you like it. I took flavors I've noticed you enjoy to make a new black tea inspired by you. It's an assam blend with vanilla and fresh orange peel, just like the dessert flavors you seem to like."

A wave of emotions broke over her, affection and joy mixing with grief. Tears pricked at her eyes, and her throat constricted. Her hands shook and she dropped the tin. Oh no. She detested when she got upset like this in front of others. She couldn't control her reactions, making it difficult to speak. And with Martin watching her, the urge to cry grew stronger from her embarrassment. She wished she was cool under pressure like Laoise. Sometimes Laoise's temper got the best of her, but her voice and body never seized up like Charlotte's.

"Let's set this down," Martin said as he plucked the teacup away and sat it down on its saucer. "I can make a new blend. Something that doesn't upset you."

She shook her head. "I l-love the tea. B-but I'm not who you think I a-am." She couldn't keep the tremors out of her voice. Or the sniffles. Her reaction made her want to run and hide where no one could see her, especially not Martin.

"You ... aren't Charlotte Graham?" He squinted at her, a frown creasing his forehead. Panic crossed his features, his eyes widening. "What did you do with Charlotte?"

"I am Charlotte."

He pulled glasses out of his pocket, one lens blue the other rose. He squinted at her as he inspected her from head to toe. "So you are." He pocketed the glasses. "But how can you be Charlotte, but also not be Charlotte?"

"That's not what I meant." She took a deep breath. "I meant I'm not nobility."

His concern fell away, replaced with a smile of relief. "I didn't think you were. I don't know of any noble families with your last name."

She wrung her hands. "It doesn't bother you that I'm not nobility?" After all this worrying for naught, she felt as though she needed to scream in frustration and relief. She'd stayed awake staring at the ceiling last night thinking about this inevitable confession. Imagining all the ways it could end in disaster. Her eyes burned and she furiously tried to blink the tears away.

"Not at all. I wouldn't care if you were a baker's daughter." He patted her hand, and no longer able to contain her emotions, she burst into tears. His eyes widened. His hands flapped around as he patted the blanket around him. As if realizing he didn't know what he was looking for, he froze. "What is wrong? What can I do to help?"

Charlotte tried to speak, but all that came out was incoherent noises and hiccups.

"Would you like your tea?" He grabbed it, but her fresh round of sobs sent his hands searching for something else. "Food? Or how about my handkerchief?" He yanked it out of his pocket and gave it to her.

She leaned forward, resting her forehead against his shoulder, balling his handkerchief in one hand and resting the other on his arm. She breathed in the soothing scent of him, focusing on it and his warmth instead of the contract poking her. He rested his head on top of hers. They stayed there for several minutes. Then finally she sucked in a deep breath to muster her courage.

"I am a baker's daughter. Clarke Bakery is my family's bakery. You've already met my mother. She works the counter, but I was too embarrassed to tell you the truth. I'm sorry." She tightened her grip on her arm and squeezed her eyes shut, afraid to look at him.

He grabbed her by the shoulders and pulled away, holding her in front of him. "Clarke Bakery? The bakery where I get my cinnamon buns?"

"Yes."

"Well, that is wonderful!" He let go and fished around for his notebook. "Do you think your parents could make our wedding cake? And some wedding cinnamon buns?"

"Erm, I suppose. But Martin—" Her voice cracked and her throat tightened. "Hawke House." As she spoke she became more and more incoherent as sobs bubbled out of her, "Bertram is going to shut it down. Please don't let him. My friend needs Hawke."

"Don't worry. I will take care of it." He reached for her tea and held it out to her. "Have your tea. It will help soothe your throat."

She accepted the tea, her hands steady enough this time to sip at it. "It's still hot," she murmured in surprise.

He nodded. "I enchanted the cups to keep the tea at the perfect drinking temperature for up to an hour. Are you sure you like the flavor? I can change it for you if you don't."

"I love the tea the way it is." She took another sip, the tea settling her emotions. "Thank you for making this. It was sweet of you." She'd never expected to inspire anything, let alone a tea flavor. No one but Martin could have blended the tea for her. As she sipped at her cup, she wondered if this was what love felt like. Warm and comforting.

"Are you sure?"

"Yes." She looked back at the tin. "And you can call me Lottie if you wish. My parents always have."

"Lottie. I like it." He grinned, the skin around his eyes crinkling from his delight. "Mar-tea and Lot-tea. It's like we were destined to drink tea together."

She laughed, her earlier worries draining away as her hands and voice steadied. "I suppose it was." He filled her cup back up. "Until I picked up The String of Pearls, I had no idea you enjoyed such terrifying stories. What draws you to them?"

She smiled, imagining the feeling a good story gave her. "Anything that makes me sit up and want to read faster while I forget the world around me. I savor that experience of getting to be scared while remaining safe." The best ones frightened her at night when the sun set and she feared what could be hiding in the dark. A good fright was as delicious as a spiced fruit roll and she could never get enough.

"I think I understand. I often forget where I am when I'm working on a new spell or a tea blend. The satisfaction of a success stays with me for days and makes me want to start a new one."

"Exactly! That is why I write too. I long to be able to give others the same wonderment I get when I read a good story."

He gave her a serious nod. "A noble pursuit. I will have to start reading more stories."

She held in her list of recommendations, knowing once she got started it would be hard to quit. Her stomach growled. "Is it time to eat yet?"

With one swift motion he yanked the lid of the basket open. He tilted the basket to let her see inside. "I brought plenty of food." His cook had filled it to the brim with fruits, cheeses, bread, and sundry other things hidden inside. "May I propose a toast before we eat?"

"Certainly."

He held up his teacup, his expression remaining serious. "To The Great Exhibition. May it be as successful as our engagement."

A successful engagement. Funny how she hadn't viewed it thus until now. If he was willing to accept her as the baker's daughter she was, then she was willing to marry him. Then she'd get to kiss him more often. And drink his delicious tea. The thought made her smile.

"To us." She clinked her teacup against his and they both drank, the hot brew leaving her warm and content. Bertram wouldn't win, she decided. Not this time. She'd find a way to yank Hawke out of his greedy hand. And keep Martin.

Chapter 16

Charlotte pinned up the stray piece of hair dangling over her shoulder. Excitement buzzed through her. The Great Exhibition! She couldn't believe it was already here. Attending alongside Martin made the engagement feel more permanent. Like Bertram couldn't tear it away from her with a kiss or a highwayman disguise.

Her hands tensed at the thought of Bertram. She hadn't seen or heard a word from him since his latest threat and that left her feeling queasy. It gave him too much time to plot and plan. If only he'd get held up by a real highwayman to teach him a lesson. As romantic as the penny blood Black Bess made Dick Turpin seem, he'd been a ruthless killer in real life. He wasn't someone Charlotte ever wanted to meet, but Bertram on the other hand ...

Martin loved Bertram. That much was clear, and it left a bad taste in the back of her mouth at the thought of being the one to open his eyes to the awful truth. For his own sake he needed to see his cousin's intentions before Bertram hurt his business or ruined their engagement for good. With that her excitement deflated. Bertram. Always the rain cloud souring her day.

Voices drifted up from the bakery below. The stairwell had a habit of echoing the noise from downstairs into the living quarters. "I can see the resemblance," a voice said. "You have the same beautiful eyes." She froze. Martin. He was early, and she hadn't planned on him meeting her parents yet. She ran down the stairs, taking them as fast as she could without tripping down them in her heels. By the time she reached the front of the bakery her mother was already giggling like a schoolgirl.

"You are too sweet," her mother gushed as Charlotte rushed to the counter. Both of them turned to her. Martin had shaved, she noted.

"Look!" Her mother held up a basket. "Mr. Steepe brought us a basket of samples from his shop. And a tin of that smoky tea! Your father is going to be thrilled. He's been out since Christmas."

"How thoughtful," Charlotte murmured, touched he'd brought them all a gift. "Father will love the tea."

Claude stepped into the front room, a small tray of cinnamon buns in his hands.

Following Martin's gaze, Charlotte murmured an introduction. Just as she finished Claude tripped over his own feet. The cinnamon buns went flying through the air. Charlotte's mother gasped and covered her eyes. Martin caught one cinnamon bun, the others landed neatly on the display tray on the counter. Charlotte and her mother both gave a sigh of relief.

"Forgive Claude," Charlotte said. "He is ... well, we think he might be cursed."

"Cursed you say? But this is exactly what I wanted." Martin shook the cinnamon bun in his hand. Then he pulled out those ridiculous glasses with colored lenses to peer at Claude. "Fascinating, he really is cursed," Martin said.

"He is? How can you tell?"

"The rune is glowing on his forehead." He tilted his head. "Read one way the rune means chaos, but the other it means baker, as if the caster laid two runes over one another and they blended together. Absolutely marvelous work. I've never seen anything like it before."

"Are you saying that I was cursed to become a baker?" Claude asked.

"A rather odd path to becoming a baker, yes, but it does seem to have worked."

Claude's mouth hung open as he stared down at the cinnamon buns. Originally he'd wanted to follow in his father's footsteps as a potter. The poor boy had a lot to come to terms with.

She tugged on Martin's sleeve. "We should get going. I don't want to miss anything."

"Of course. Perhaps soon your family can come over for dinner. The garden is almost in full bloom." He tucked his glasses back into his pocket.

"That would be lovely. I'd love to come over and see the garden," her mother said. "Just tell us when and we'll be there." That smile and fawning meant her mother was already pleased with Martin. And Charlotte knew that meant her father wouldn't object. Then again, at her age, her father wasn't likely to object to anyone with money willing to marry her. And thanks to the Lapsang tea he'd be as enamored with Martin as her mother was.

They stepped out into the chilly morning air. A light mist clung to her street, reminding her of their dances. She smiled at the memory. Martin held out a hand to help her into the carriage and she gave his hand a squeeze as she climbed in. Martin settled in across from her. Beside him sat a tall object hidden beneath cloth.

"I got you what you asked for at the picnic. I was worried I wouldn't have it in time for today, but I managed without a minute to spare."

"You did?" Had Bertram confessed to his sabotage? Agreed to back down? Or sell Hawke back? That would explain why she hadn't heard any new threats from him.

He pulled the cloth away, revealing a gray bird with yellow eyes and a brown and white striped chest.

Confusion fell over Charlotte. For the life of her she couldn't figure out what the bird had to do with anything.

"I wasn't sure what type of hawk you preferred exactly, but this is the only one I managed to capture in the gardens. I believe it's a sparrowhawk. I can have birdhouses built within the week. Do you have a preference on color for those?" His voice stayed even and matter-of-fact, as if this was business as normal for him. He even reached for his notebook.

"I ... erm ... I don't understand. Why do you have a hawk in a cage?" She clasped her hands together, squeezing her nerves away.

He blinked at her. "Is that not what you wanted? When you were crying you said you wanted a hawk house. My mother already has birdhouses for songbirds in the garden. One for a hawk shouldn't be much trouble to add."

Realization dawned and Charlotte slapped a hand to her forehead in exasperation. "I didn't mean the bird. I was talking about Hawke Publishing House and Bertram." Still, part of her found it sweet that he was willing to go to such lengths for her, softening her frustration.

Martin frowned. "Then I think I misunderstood most of what you said. I thought you wanted a birdhouse for a hawk." He glanced down at the bird and cleared his throat. "Do you not want this then?"

"No. I don't know what I'd do with a hawk, but I do appreciate the thought."

He nodded. "I understand. I should have asked for clarification." The carriage stopped behind a line of carriages heading toward the Crystal Palace. Martin opened the carriage door and then the cage. The hawk flew out, a woman on the sidewalk screaming as it soared past her. Martin closed the door. "Can you explain again? What exactly about Hawke House is the problem?"

"It is my friend's family business, but her uncle made off with most of the money and now it has been struggling. Bertram bought it, and I fear he plans to shut it down. He seems upset over our engagement. He thinks ... he thinks you should marry into nobility. And that I only wanted you to get you to invest in Hawke." She squeezed her hands tighter, hating the way insecurity flooded her. "I can explain more after our visit to The Great Exhibition, but all I want is for him to not shut Hawke down."

Martin rubbed the back of his neck as he considered her words. "That makes a lot more sense than what I thought you'd said when you were crying. I'm not surprised that he is upset over the engagement. He was always protective when we were children, and to this day he seems to see threats everywhere. I already made him promise to not kiss you, but I'll speak to him again about Hawke." He jotted down a note in his notebook before putting it away.

"That is good. When you drop me off at home, I'll fetch the contract he showed me. I was hoping you might be able to do something to help Hawke. Give them some advice perhaps or connect them with possible investors."

Martin shifted in his seat, chewing on his bottom lip. "I will take a look at it and see if I can help."

"No real hawks this time."

He gave her an embarrassed smile. "No hawks."

"Did you really capture that bird just for me?"

"I did. It seemed an odd request, but if it was what would make you happy again, I was determined to do it. I suppose I won't have to put that birdhouse order in with the carpenter today."

"It is sweet that you were willing to do that for me."

"I'm sorry." He sighed as he moved the bird cage out of the way. "I do have a knack for misunderstanding and making a mess of romance. I've always thought that's what drove her into Bertram's arms instead of mine." His face crumpled and Charlotte didn't need to ask to understand who he was referring to. His last fiancée. "But business, I can do. I will see to Hawke's situation and what can be done for them."

"You are sweet and thoughtful, even when you misunderstand." She thought back to his mother's warning to be clear with him. She understood now. But a fiancé willing to catch her a hawk just to make her happy, that was more than worth all his faults.

The carriage door opened. Martin hopped out first and offered a hand to help her out. The Crystal Palace gleamed in the morning light. She couldn't think of a better descriptor for it than a palace due to its immense size and all those shining panels of glass. As they headed inside she couldn't help but to crane her head upward, marveling at how tall the building was. As amazing as she found the outside, it couldn't compete with the inside. Her breath caught on the sight of the large fountain and the trees they'd built the palace around. Mixed with all the glass and the awe-inspiring height of the palace, she almost felt like she wasn't indoors at all.

Exhibition displays lined the walkway with a second row on top of the first ending in balconies that overlooked the main floor. Two men strolled by, speaking what she guessed to be German. Behind them she caught bits of French and ahead of them a language she couldn't begin to guess at.

"This is amazing." She didn't know where to look first. As soon as her gaze alighted on one display, another distracted her away.

"We'll have to be sure to see the Koh-i-Noor diamond. I heard it mentioned several times at the party. Everyone was curious to see it."

"It will take all day to see everything! How many exhibits are there?"

"About 13,000."

She sucked in her breath at the number. "Make that a week. I thought there would be a few hundred displays, not thousands." She'd expected boring business displays, instead colorful displays of anything and everything she could think of surrounded them. "I can't imagine all the planning Prince Albert put into this."

He looked up as they passed a towering elm tree. "When you can build something this magnificent with technology, I understand why people think we don't need magic. Still, it makes me wonder what the two could do combined. We could make even more unimaginable wonders."

They walked past a long line and she craned her neck to see past. "The Koh-i-Noor line is long. I wonder if it is really that impressive."

"It is the world's largest diamond. I bet everyone wants to get a look at it."

She pictured a diamond the size of her head, but she could see nothing past the line. Right before they reached the sign for refreshments, they passed a large telescope. She paused to admire it, having to jog to catch back up with Martin, but there was yet more that drew her attention.

"Let me show you the shop and check in with Arjun. Then I would love to look at the other exhibits with you."

"Arjun!" She snapped her fingers. "I meant to tell you how kind he was to me when I thought I was being followed. I appreciated his help."

"I am not surprised. He is very popular with my customers. I could have not made my shop such a success without him, and I hope he works his talents here as well." The tantalizing scent of pastries and grilled meats floated through the air, growing stronger with each step. "Here we are."

Trees added to the park feel of the refreshment room, including one across from Martin's little shop. They brought attention to just how tall the Crystal Palace was. The tea shop counter was situated at the back of the stall with shelves sticking out, forming the sides to display the colorful tins of tea available for customers to browse. Behind the counter sat Martin's new tea set and kettle in several different designs, a sign proclaiming the magical tea ware was available for order and would pour itself, keep the cup at the perfect drinking temperature, and that the kettle boiled water twice as fast as a stove. A large rug gave the space between the shelves the feeling of a calming little oasis among all the excitement and crowds filling the Crystal Palace.

Martin chatted with Arjun while she explored the cozy little pop-up shop. She stepped between the shelves to approach the counter. The shelves blocked the distracting view of the other exhibits, allowing her to focus on the tea. A stack of business cards listing the shop's address decorated the counter. And there on a small pedestal down the counter from Arjun rested Lu Yu's talking teapot. She didn't need to see anything else to know this would be her favorite exhibit. Nothing could match the pride thrumming through her or the warmth she felt when she spotted Charlotte's tea on the menu.

In the past when she thought of courtship she'd imagined long walks through Hyde Park and carriage rides. Not this.

A couple stepped up to the little shop, fawning over all the tea options. When they made it to the counter, Louie launched into his introduction, steam pouring from his spout.

"I am the ancient teapot of Lu Yu." He droned on as the man gawked and the woman squealed in surprise. Her reaction drew the attention of a family walking past. They paused, the parents discussing in quick whispers before coming over to look at the shop's offerings.

Martin filled a kettle before sneaking out from behind the counter. He handed Charlotte a milky cup of tea. "Arjun's vanilla chai," he explained. "It will keep us warm while we walk."

She sipped at it, the warmth helping fight off the chill of the morning. Cardamom and cinnamon burst on her tongue. "Delicious. I could drink this every morning."

"I have it every time I visit my shop. I have yet to perfect it like Arjun, and I doubt I could match his skills at it."

The tea shop's stall grew more popular by the minute. Martin paused, smiling at the gathering crowd. "This is a good start. If all goes well this will help me get my tea stocked in more countries. I'd like to find some American businesses to connect with."

"I'm glad it's already going well for you." She squeezed the cup of chai, enjoying the tea's warmth on her cold hands. The sweetness of the decadent vanilla made her sigh in delight. "I'm certain everyone who tries your tea will love it." She breathed in the heavenly aroma of the chai. "Louie seems to be a hit as well." A group of children gathered around, listening to the teapot tell a story.

He nodded as he sipped at his chai. "Can you believe I gave him away once? I donated him to a museum in China, figuring he belonged back home."

"If you sent him home, then why do you still have him?"

"Because the museum sent it back. They said they had other, quieter teapots that belonged to Lu Yu and didn't need any others. Something must have gone wrong with the translation because the museum curator called the teapot annoying and said it distracted from the other displays with its 'incessant babbling.' I think he's rather charming, don't you?"

Charlotte smiled. "Perhaps they simply couldn't appreciate him like you do."

He gave her a gentle look of affection. "I'm grateful for your support, and that you came today. It has meant more to me than I could ever put into words."

"There is nowhere else I'd rather be."

Their eyes connected and he stroked her cheek. "How about we start with the Koh-i-Noor before your lips distract me too much? I'm curious to see how big it is."

She laughed. "Lead on."

Chapter 17

"That's it?" Charlotte asked as they peered down at the diamond. "That isn't even as big as my fist. I was expecting ... a lot more." The sign of the oval diamond claimed it was one hundred and five carats. She wasn't quite sure what that meant, but she didn't care after seeing how small the diamond was. In the time it'd taken for them to reach the front of the line, she'd already finished her chai. She craved another cup, but with thousands of exhibits to go, she didn't want to waste time. His hand brushed hers and she smiled. To touch in a place this public felt forbidden, and that made it all the more exciting.

Martin squinted at the diamond. "It is disappointing. I expected it to be bigger." They moved aside, letting the next people in line have a closer look.

"That's it?" the woman said as she stepped up to the display.

"Bertram's exhibit should be down this way." Martin pointed to the left. "His prototype didn't make it in time for the opening, but he has other rifles on display."

"How about that one instead?" Charlotte made for the closest exhibit to their right. She couldn't tell what it was thanks to the people blocking her view, but all that mattered was that it was away from Bertram's. Today was not a day she wanted him to attempt to ruin her life yet again. Without him sticking his chiseled jaw in the way, she felt comfortable at Martin's side. And hopeful.

"There is a printing press somewhere as well. I thought you might like to see how books are printed."

"I would love that. I never put much thought to how books are made beyond the writing of them." She bet Mary already knew all about printing presses after growing up amongst all of Hawke's books. A stab of envy tried to worm its way into her chest and she shoved it away. She wouldn't trade the bakery for anything. Not even books.

"The Tara Brooch," she said, reading the display sign, "by George Waterhouse. It's from the early eighth century. It's Celtic."

That got Martin's attention. "Is it at all magical? The Celts had some interesting enchantments I've longed to study."

"No, but it's pretty." The gold filigree panels on the silver brooch reflected the sun shining through the glass walls of the palace.

"That brooch looks off," Martin said, leaning closer to the glass. "Isn't it meant to have studs in it? It doesn't match the description." He pulled his odd pair of glasses out of his pocket and clipped on two extra lenses that stuck out on either side of the glasses, one blue and one rose. They reminded her of the awful contraption he'd been wearing when she first called on him in his study shortly after their announced engagement.

He slid the extra lenses in front of the glasses, his attention absorbed by the brooch. A little girl ran up to peer at the brooch, then ran right back off again to the next exhibit, her younger brother toddling past in a hurry as he struggled to keep up.

"Are those reading glasses? Or something else?"

He pushed the blue lens aside and then the rose one before going back to the blue. Then he pulled yet another lens from his pocket, this one amber. He clipped off the rose lens and replaced it with the new one. Charlotte bit her bottom lip to keep from laughing at how silly he looked.

"Magic reading glasses to be precise. They can see through glamour and let me see magic in general. They make enchanting easier and are great for studying enchanted objects. This is my portable pair. I have a full set in my study."

"I didn't know there was such a thing. What do you see?"

"It looks as though a plain brooch was glamoured to look like the Tara Brooch. I suppose they were afraid to put the real one on display. They should however have hired a better magician. This glamour looks rushed. It won't last the day."

Charlotte took a second look, noticing how fuzzy the filigree lines looked upon closer inspection. "That is going to disappoint a lot of people later." It still wouldn't be as disappointing as the diamond though.

They moved on, going from exhibit to exhibit. They took extra time at the exhibit of stuffed kittens taking tea sent by the German Customs Union. "They are fuzzy and adorable," Martin crooned. "Cuter than teddy bears even. This is the best exhibit." He leaned closer, mouth parted slightly as he watched them.

Charlotte giggled at how entranced he was. Whatever enchantment was on them caused them to lift their teacups up and down as though they were drinking. "The magic is as finely crafted as everything else." When he turned to wondering if the exhibit was for sale, she pulled him on. They passed Matthew Brady's daguerreotypes, several of them enchanted to move like Roquefort's paintings. A stiff man in a suit blinked up at them from one image. Then a somber couple with a child squeezing a teddy bear. Martin lingered at the moving ones. "The magic has been altered from what is commonly used on paintings to fit the format. Very clever."

She got the feeling he would be wearing those ridiculous glasses the whole time. At least with so many exhibits to look at, no one spared him more than a glance. She considered asking him to remove them and then thought better of it. If they were to marry, it was better to get used to such things. Except she couldn't look at his face without risking bursting into giggles.

"There is a lot of magic around the Daria-i-Noor." Martin flicked his lenses back and forth.

They moved into the short line and a minute later stepped up to the pink diamond.

"It looks like a pink rock." Charlotte tilted her head, but every which way she looked at it all she saw was a rock.

"That's because it is a rock glamoured to be pink. Can't anyone afford a good magician for glamour?" He threw up his hands in exasperation. "It's the most popular magic in Britain. There are plenty of women and men who know it better than this."

"I wasn't expecting faux displays. Are many of the other exhibits using glamour as well?"

Martin glanced around and up at the balconies. "I see glamour near the displays from India near the gold ornaments. And down there in the American exhibits there is lingering magic that is very fresh."

"May I borrow those glasses?"

He handed them to her and she put them on. At first it was disorienting for half the world to turn blue and the other half amber. After a moment she grew used to the tinted world. She turned her attention back to the diamond to get her bearings and just as Martin had said, she saw nothing but a rock through a mist of white magic.

"It's odd, isn't it? For them to be putting fake displays out." She wished she understood magic as well as Martin did. It could be another connection between them, one she wanted to explore and learn more about. Later she could teach him more about baking. Or penny bloods.

"I don't agree with it." Martin folded his hands behind his back. "It goes against what the exhibition stands for when to comes to showing off these goods to the world, but I don't think we can do anything about it."

"I'm curious about the glamour in the American displays if it is the most recent. Can we head there next?"

They set off, glancing at the exhibits they passed on the way. The sheer amount was dizzying from jewelry displays to furniture and inventions. The trail ended at Samuel Colt's gun exhibit display of pistols and revolvers. "None of the guns have been glamoured, except for that one." She pointed at a pistol wrapped in a cloud of magic. She removed the blue lens, using the amber to get a better look at the blue enchantment wrapped around the gun. Threads of magic wrapped around it in a pattern that reminded her of lace.

"The Colt Navy. I couldn't say why. Guns are my uncle and Bertram's sphere of knowledge. I've never even been hunting before."

"I don't know anything about guns either, but I had no idea magic looked like that. It looks delicate."

"Beautiful, isn't it? Good magic takes a good craftsman like any other work."

"It is." A burst of fresh excitement tingled down her spine. These glasses made her feel like a detective in a penny blood serial. And if those serials had taught her anything, there was always something interesting to be found at the end of a clue trail. She turned, sweeping her gaze up and down the aisle of displays. Multiple trails converged on the main walkway in a spiderweb going from exhibit to exhibit. She followed the point where the trail converged. "The magic is strongest this way." They backtracked as she followed alongside the magic, dodging excited children and couples walking arm in arm. The trail held steady as they approached a refreshment room.

Her stomach dropped when she saw where the trail went. "Are you using glamour at your shop?"

"No. I have enchantments on the teaware, but no glamour. You'd need the rose lens to see the enchantments." He pulled it from his pocket and switched it out with the amber lens. "See it?"

A fog of magic hovered in the shop, intersecting with the trail showing on the blue lens. "I see it." She took a few more steps forward, confirming her fears. "The magic trail leads to your shop. But if the glamour isn't yours, then whose is it?"

Chapter 18

"There shouldn't be any magic but my own at the shop." Martin's lips pressed together in worry.

"You don't think there is a thief on the loose, do you? Is there anything valuable someone would want to steal?"

Martin thought a moment. Then horror broke over his face, widening his eyes. "Louie!" he cried before running to his shop. Charlotte ran after him, dodging around a man with both hands full of Schwepps drinks. At first glance nothing looked out of the ordinary at the tea shop. The short line moved quickly as Arjun served customers. The shelves of tea tins remained tidy and Lu Yu's teapot was still on the counter. Based on his droning voice, he hadn't been replaced. Not yet anyway. Yet the lightest mist of glamour hung in the air behind the counter near Martin's enchantments.

She headed behind the counter and checked the large bag of Earl Grey, finding nothing but tea leaves. Martin checked on Louie, the teapot ignoring his wandering hands as he rambled on to a child staring at the teapot in wonderment. Relief and disappointment mixed together, relief that the shop was all right and disappointment at there being no discovery at the end of the trail. It felt like the adventure to the docks, like she'd stepped into the clothes of a detective for several minutes, but now she was back to simply being Charlotte. Not that she didn't enjoy being herself, but the chance to escape into something different felt exhilarating.

She reached for the nearest teapot, a brown porcelain with delicate swirls of white throughout.

"Do you like it?" Martin stepped up beside her.

"Yes. How do you activate the magic?"

"Heat activates it. For the kettle the heat of the fire, for this the heat of the tea activates the runes. It makes magic accessible to those with no magical knowledge. Your enchantment was the final puzzle piece because it was exactly what I needed to make my idea work."

"I ... that is amazing." Such a simple thing, but the kettle would be a time saver. Her mother would love one in the morning when the rush started as soon as they opened their doors and every second counted. More than once she'd given up on the kettle knowing there wasn't enough time. The rich wouldn't notice the difference when they left tea to the maids, but the common folk would appreciate the time savings.

She opened the lid to get a closer look at the design. Something inside gleamed. She reached inside and pulled out a pink stone. "What is this?"

"That looks like a diamond." He put the diamond and lid back before opening the next teapot. This time he lifted a brooch out. "And this looks like the Tara Brooch! Goodness, what is it doing here?" He put it back and stepped behind the curtain backdrop of the shop to pace. She followed him. Behind him the glass wall showed them Hyde Park. "Someone must have hidden them here for a reason. But why inside my teapots?"

Charlotte considered her list of suspects. Martin had been with her all morning, leaving no time for him to make his way around the Crystal Palace alone and steal. Arjun had his hands busy with customers. And Louie, well, he didn't have any hands being a teapot and all. From there, her list was blank. With people from all over the world walking the palace, any number of politics could be at play. She'd never been one for keeping up with politics.

"Hello, Martin," a voice spat out.

They whirled to find a man standing between them and the curtain. A thick mist of magic surrounded his face, but the jaw stuck out. "You," she hissed as she ripped the glasses off. The glamour gave the man a hairy mole on his cheek and a crooked nose far too big for his face. A hat hid his hair, but nothing could hide his thick bushy eyebrows that looked like caterpillars. His perfect jaw remained untouched.

"Yes, you there, what do you want?" Martin asked, irritation coating his words.

The man waved the pistol in his hand, keeping it close to his side. "I'm here to catch you in the act of thieving. Don't move, either of you." He'd done nothing to change his voice. He sounded the same as always.

Martin scoffed in offense. "Thieving? I would never!"

"Except you have. You've stolen valuables from all over the exhibition and hidden them in your teapots. You've stolen the Tara Brooch, the Daria-i-Noor, and a number of other valuable jewels and gems. The police will be here soon ,and you'll be arrested for your thefts."

"I didn't do any of that." Martin's hands flew up. "None of it! And I resent being accused."

"He did it, Martin," Charlotte held in her sigh at how oblivious he could be. "He's framing you for the thefts. Your innocence doesn't matter to him." Really, would it hurt him to read a few more penny bloods about detectives and criminals to learn about these things?

Martin froze, blinking in surprise. "Why would this hideously ugly man want to frame me?"

"I'm not ugly," the man snapped. "And you are unbelievably dense sometimes." He mumbled a string of Latin and the glamour fell away except for the large, crooked nose.

"Bertie!" Martin gasped out. "You are getting better at glamour, but you continue to go overboard with it."

Bertram's nostrils flared and his left eyebrow twitched.

The curtain rustled and Arjun poked his head out. "Mr. Steepe, would you like another cup of tea?" Betram tightened his grip on the pistol, turning his body slightly to hide it from Arjun's eyes.

Martin lifted a finger. "Oh yes, another chai please."

"Martin!" Charlotte cried.

"Sorry, would you like one too? How about you, Bertram?"

Both of them stared at him. Their silence didn't faze him. He lifted two more fingers. "Three cups of chai, please."

"Right away, sir." Arjun ducked back into the tea shop.

"You aren't taking this seriously, are you?" Bertram asked.

Martin crossed his arms. "I think you've taken your joke a little too far, and I don't see the humor in it. You can return everything on your own."

Bertram scowled, a vein throbbing in his forehead. "This isn't a joke. You are going to jail for stealing valuable artifacts."

Martin frowned, forehead wrinkling as he processed Bertram's words.

"Why are you framing him?" Charlotte demanded. "He is your cousin. He's done nothing to you."

"He is squandering his talents and his inheritance on a tea shop. Ridiculous! How is a tea shop and a side hobby publishing magical books going to look after our family? And to marry you when he should be aiming for a title. Pitiful. The Steepes could become nobility. I could marry my sisters off to earls and viscounts. But everything I've done to convince him away from this farce has failed. I've been left with no choice but to make sure he can't do anything at all before he ruins the whole family."

Martin chewed on the inside of his cheek. He wasn't quite convinced, Charlotte thought. But she could help him see his cousin's treachery.

"The warehouse fire was you, wasn't it? As was the explosion on the ship I bet. And you were Dick Turpin, trying to steal Martin's new teapot. You've been attacking his business this whole time."

"At least one of you is clever enough to see the truth."

Martin's gaze fell to the floor, arms dropping to his sides. "I've always tried to think the best of you, Bertie." His voice came out quiet. "You are the last person I'd want to see as an enemy. I thought you were having bad luck with all those misfortunes."

Charlotte reached for his arm, giving it a gentle squeeze. "They weren't misfortunes at all. Bertram betrayed your trust."

"They weren't simple misfortunes," Bertram agreed, "but none of them went as planned. That ship explosion cost me my prototype thanks to you, Cousin. That, paired with the warehouse fire that ruined my stock of fabric, has cost me all but my Chinese investor for my rifle business."

"You have a Chinese investor?" Martin's head rose, his curiosity piqued. "I didn't know that."

"I do. A company called Lapsang Limited. With them I will save our family from your poor choices. I will make sure everyone is well looked after."

Martin's frown deepened. "Lapsang is my investment company. I have shares in all your business ventures."

Bertram's reddening cheeks puffed in outrage. "You?"

"Yes, I named it after my favorite tea. It's the company I made when Father urged me to start my own business dealings. I used Lapsang's profits to fund my tea shop. I told you about it when I set it up. You even gave me some advice."

"You never told me the name," Bertram hissed. "I thought you were running part of your father's business, not creating your own."

"You never asked, and I didn't want to rely on you too much. I wanted to handle the business myself to prove to Father I was capable."

Bertram spluttered. Charlotte glanced between the men, wishing she could take Martin's pain away. He loved his cousin too much to turn on him, and that meant she would need to step up. For Martin, she would protect him.

"This plan of yours was sneaky." She stepped closer to Bertram, keeping her movements slow and her hands up. "You should never hide your good looks beneath glamour."

He scoffed. "You think I'm going to believe that act of yours?"

"What act?" She batted her eyelashes and ran a hand down his arm. "You've clearly won. Why not another kiss to celebrate? Every woman in the ballroom was envious of me that night."

Martin stiffened, hurt swimming in his eyes. "Do you really mean that? Do you prefer him?"

Bertram's brow rose. He smirked. "Please, do continue, Miss Graham." He emphasized her name. "Tell Martin more about our kiss."

Martin made a noise of indignation in his throat. His hands balled.

Charlotte wanted to punch Bertram. Instead she kept a fake smile plastered on as she climbed her hand back up his arm. She crept closer. "No woman could possibly resist you." She moved a single finger over his bicep, her mind focusing on the mistake she made in the runes on the swan boat. The tilt of one rune was all she needed.

Martin's face turned pink. "Stealing Charlotte is going too far, Bertram. I challenge you to a duel." Martin jabbed a finger toward Bertram's chest.

"A duel, really? I'm the one holding a gun here." He shook the gun.

"Find a second one for me, and we can meet out on the lawn! We can do it right here in Hyde Park."

"You've never even held a gun, Martin. Much less shot one. And you'd be willing to throw your life away for a girl this fickle! Can't you see she's turned her back on you to save herself?"

Martin's face turned purple as though he forgot to breathe.

Charlotte whispered the spell and smoke drifted from Bertram's coat quickly followed by a flame.

"But I won't be as easily fooled as you were by this act. Face it, ever since your sickness you've become a blunderbuss. This is for your own good as much as it is for the fam—" Bertram's head jerked toward his arm as a single flame spread toward his shoulder. He yelped and dropped the pistol. Charlotte dove for it while he ripped his coat off and threw it to the ground where he stomped the flames out. Charlotte backed up, standing in front of Martin, pistol raised at Bertram.

"Lottie?" Martin whispered, his voice a mix of hope and confusion.

"I'm not letting him get away with this. He can go to jail for his own crimes."

Martin clasped his hands together behind his back. "I see no other recourse. You are right. Arjun," he raised his voice, "please make sure the constables find their way to us."

"Yes, sir," Arjun's voice drifted through the curtain.

A whistle from nearby told them the bobbies were coming.

Bertram snickered. "I'm not the one with a stolen pistol in my hands, am I? Thank you for your help, Miss Graham."

An officer burst through the curtain and another one appeared from the narrow alleyway between the shop and its neighbor.

Bertram's smile disappeared. He put on a look of fear. "Help! She threatened to shoot me! They've both stolen valuables and hid them in the teapots!" The corners of his mouth twitched as he fought to suppress a smile. "My cousin's gone mad!"

"He's lying," Charlotte cried. "He's the thief! He's trying to set us up." She dropped the gun. Fury burned bright inside her. If Bertram won, he'd better hope she went to jail too or next time she pointed a pistol at him, she'd make sure to shoot.

The first policeman, a large older man with red cheeks and a bushy mustache, rolled his eyes.

"Please leave the lady out of this," Martin said. "This is between my cousin and I."

"Names, please," the younger officer said as he pulled out a notepad.

"Mr. Steepe," Bertram and Martin said at the same time.

The young man sighed. "First names."

"Bertram."

"Martin."

A third bobby appeared, a lanky redhead.

"Paul, check to see what all is inside these teapots," the older constable said, evidently the captain.

Paul got to work on emptying the teapots, pulling out one stolen valuable after another.

"I saw him putting stolen goods in his teapots." Bertram wagged a finger at Martin. "When I confronted him his fiancée turned a pistol on me."

"Liar! He had the pistol first because he stole the valuables. That is why I set his coat on fire to make him drop it." She kicked at the coat with her right foot. "See?"

The captain hummed in thought, fiddling with his mustache.

"She attacked me," Bertram argued. "She tried to burn me alive!"

"Why would I attack you if I already had the gun?" Charlotte countered. "And why would I bring a gun if I thought I could burn you alive? I merely did a small spell to make you drop the gun so you couldn't shoot us."

The younger bobby nodded as he jotted down notes.

"We should take this elsewhere and question them individually," the captain said. "Paul, see if you can find any witnesses. We need an outside account to verify who stole what."

"I heard everything," a voice said, drawing out the words.

"What was that?" The captain asked as he turned to Arjun who peered out of the curtain.

Arjun shook his head. "That wasn't me. I didn't see anything except Mr. Steepe poking around the teapots."

When the officer with the notepad looked up expectantly, Arjun pointed to Bertram. The man nodded and made another note.

"I heard everything," the voice from before said. "Every last word and I can recount to you." The bobbies all looked about, but no other person appeared.

"Down here," the teapot of Lu Yu said as Arjun pulled the curtain aside.

"A teapot?" Paul said.

"I am the teapot of Lu Yu, the author of The Classic of Tea." Louie said, launching into his introduction, "The book includes—"

"Absurd," Bertram said, cutting off Louie. "A teapot can't be a witness to a crime. It's a teapot. He doesn't have eyes! How can he see?"

"Magic," Martin said.

"I have been a witness in four previous trials. I will list them now."

Perplexed, the captain scratched at his mustache while he listened. Once Louie concluded his list, the man shrugged. "Well there's no law that says a teapot can't be a witness. And there seems to be precedent."

"Please have a seat and I will recount the tale of the stolen exhibition valuables. This tale interconnects with several others that all led to this day."

"Good enough for me," the large constable said. "Paul, keep an eye on these three. Patrick, keep taking notes."

With Arjun's help Paul grabbed a table for their use in front of the teashop. They all settled around the table and Arjun served them all fresh tea.

"I don't want to sit and listen to a teapot." Bertram crossed his arms. Paul shoved him down onto a chair. Bertram's sour expression pleased Charlotte. He deserved to squirm.

"Excellent tea," the captain said. Milk foam clung to his mustache.

"Thank you," Martin said, beginning to perk up. "The tea is available to purchase as are my new teapots and kettles. Please feel free to visit my main shop as well." He plucked a business card from his pocket and handed it to the constable.

The captain pocketed the card. "I should take some Earl Grey home. My wife can never get enough of it."

"Please do," Martin said.

Then Arjun set Louie down in the center of the table and the tale began. Charlotte reached for Martin's hand.

"This tale begins on the morning of May first, 1851 before the opening ceremony to The Great Exhibition. The time was six twenty-three in the morning. A chill hung in the air as Martin Steepe finished brewing a morning cup of Lapsang Souchong, declaring the occasion special enough for the flavor ..."

"Excuse me, but I seem to be running out of steam." The teapot laughed and Martin joined in. Everyone else leaned back as the tension of the story fled.

"He has made that joke three times now!" Bertram said, slapping a hand down on the table. His abandoned tea sat in front of him, untouched since he'd pushed the first cup away.

"Yes, and it's still funny!"

Arjun returned to pour more hot water into the teapot.

The captain finished his cup, the third since the teapot's story began. He rubbed his large stomach. "I've never had better tea."

Charlotte stretched her neck, working a kink out of it from sitting. The teapot had already deviated from the day's events multiple times to go down several rabbit holes including the encounter with Dick Turpin. By the time he finished the side stories, Charlotte had almost forgotten what they were waiting to hear. Meanwhile, the exhibits went on, and Arjun continued serving customers. Their large group gathered around attracted customers to the shop out of curiosity instead of repelling them. Somehow Arjun kept up with all the customers, his energy never flagging. Charlotte itched to join him after sitting through all the stories. Her toes tapped against the ground.

"Now where was I?" the teapot said.

"We've already been sitting here for three hours," Betram complained. "How much longer is this going to take?"

"Ah, yes," the teapot continued, ignoring him. "The man with poorly done glamour returned to the tea shop twice to hide stolen valuables inside them."

"The glamour was not poorly done!" Bertram slapped his hands down on the table again.

The captain arched an eyebrow at him. "Is that your confession?"

"No, but I refuse to sit here for another three hours to listen to a porcelain teapot insult me." He paused before correcting himself, "...I mean the perpetrator. Whoever he may be."

"The first time he hid stolen jewels and gems from India," the teapot continued. "This is the third time these particular jewels were stolen this century, the first of which—"

"Enough!" Bertram shot out of his seat. Then he grabbed the table and flipped it. "Louie!" Martin shouted as he dropped to the floor to catch the teapot, who continued his story as if the table hadn't been upended right under him.

Bertram threw a ball to the ground and smoke poured from it. Charlotte squeezed her eyes shut and turned her back to the smoke bomb. A moment later she opened one eye. Behind her Bertram coughed.

"He's getting away, sir" Patrick said as he furiously scribbled down notes, now standing since his chair was trapped beneath the table.

His boss held his empty teacup in one hand, still seated. "Paul, stop the man and arrest him."

Charlotte turned. Bertram crawled away through the smoke, but the smoke did little to hide him, not even reaching his shoulders. People wandering past tittered at the spreading smoke in excited voices. Children screamed in delight. Between his coughing and his back and head sticking out of the smoke, Bertram was easy to spot.

Paul set off after Bertram at a brisk walk. Martin picked up the smoke bomb, turning it round and round. He shook his head. "This is similar to the enchantment Roquefort used on his dance floor." He poked one of the runes. "Bertie inscribed the last run incorrectly. He halved the amount of smoke instead of doubling it. Goodness, if he'd succeeded the smoke would be over our heads by now."

Paul caught up with Bertram, stepping into his path. Bertram bumped against the man's legs and tried to go around, another coughing fit wracking his frame. The officer shifted, blocking his path again. He reached for his set of handcuffs. Bertram stopped and looked around. Then he stood, dusting off his knees. The smoke pooled around his ankles. "That was not a confession."

"You've left us with no choice but to arrest you, sir."

Bertram didn't fight. He kept his poise all the while, glaring at Martin every chance he got.

Martin pulled out his glasses as he studied the ball. "A small correction here should fix it," Martin mumbled as he ran his etching pen over it. A fresh puff of smoke spewed from it.

"Martin," Charlotte cried, "make it stop!"

Martin spluttered as the smoke blew into his face. He shut the ball, putting an end to the smoke. He pocketed it before bending down to help Patrick right the table. Charlotte righted the chairs. Martin moved Louie back to the table, Louie not once stopping his story. He was now in the midst of recounting the conversation between Bertram and Martin before Charlotte set Bertram's coat on fire. Arjun returned with new cups and tea.

Paul marched Bertram back over to the table. Bertram scoffed as he was pushed back into his chair.

"We aren't staying here, are we?"

"No one is going anywhere until the witness is finished," the captain declared, "and not until I finish my tea."

Bertram groaned.

"Would you like more tea, Bertie?" Martin asked.

Betram settled his scathing look on his cousin. "I've always preferred coffee."

Martin's face fell, a somber air overtaking him. "Today truly is a dark day. I never knew you were hiding this many secrets from me."

"Yes, well you've won as you always do. Though I'll never understand it. You can keep wasting your good sense on this tea business and your commoner." He shot Charlotte a look of distaste, his nose scrunching.

"It isn't a waste at all," Charlotte said. "So be quiet. I don't want to miss the best part of the story."

"... and then fire burst from his coat."

Charlotte smiled. She'd treasure that shocked look on Bertram's face when he noticed the fire forever.

Chapter 19

The autumn air blew in through the open window, carrying the briny spray of the ocean with it. She'd need to close it soon before the breeze made the seaside cottage too cold, but for now she enjoyed the salty scent and the call of the seagulls. She set aside the newspaper declaring The Great Exhibition a success. Prince Albert had already announced he planned to use the profits to fund museums. She thought it a grand use of the money.

A seagull landed on the windowsill, and Oolong perked up. He climbed to his feet in the doorway and trotted over. The gull cried again and Oolong barked, scaring the bird off. Oolong looked pleased with himself as he laid down right on her toes, giving her a look that seemed to say "I saved you."

She poured hot cream over chocolate to make the ganache, the final touch on her new tart. This dish had been stuck in her mind all day as she sipped on Charlotte's tea. A row of Steepe Co. tea tins lined a shelf behind her. Martin had included all of her favorites and several of his own.

They were only planning on two weeks at the seaside cottage for their honeymoon, but Martin had brought two months' worth of tea plus his new kettle. He'd barely been able to keep up with the demand for his tea at The Great Exhibition, and he'd received thousands of orders for his tea ware since. And on top of all that, he'd made business connections with stores who wanted to stock his products across Europe and America. Charlotte's Tea was his latest bestseller.

Thinking about it all filled her with fleeting pride. Of course she'd been happy for Martin's success. But as their wedding came and went on the last day of The Great Exhibition and he brought her to this cozy cottage, she found herself longing to write again, to be something more than Martin Steepe's wife and a baker's daughter.

Of all the adventures she'd bumbled into this year, there had to be inspiration somewhere. No more bakery stories. She needed to think wider.

She stirred the chocolate then prepared to pour it over her tart. She'd always liked her father's bakewell tarts well enough, but raspberry jam was never a favorite of hers. This time she used orange marmalade on the crust instead. It would add a citrus note to the tart to pair with the almond frangipane and chocolate on top of it.

As she worked, she mulled over the notes from Mary she'd brought with her. Mary claimed her last book was good. Good, but too similar to The String of Pearls. But she'd loved the recipe notes Charlotte had accidentally included at the end. It'd been research for one of the dishes mentioned in the book. Mary had made the recipe herself and now she wanted to know if Charlotte had other recipes to share.

With no new ideas for her next book, she focused on her tart, hoping baking would inspire her. Maybe she should switch to cookbooks and teach readers how to make the perfect breads and pies. But baking wouldn't be enough. It never was. Even now her mind wandered as she finished the tart, searching for any thread of an idea. Funny how her mother had spent the last month worrying how Charlotte would handle getting married, but the big question of her writing left little room to worry about anything else.

Besides, Martin had never given her reason to worry. The time she'd spent strolling through the Crystal Palace, picnicking, and visiting book stores with him had given her plenty of time to adapt to his style of needing things to be said plainly instead of hinted at. She barely thought about it anymore. Although the way he smiled at her still sent butterflies swooping through her.

She scooted the tart away from the edge of the counter. Oolong rolled off her toes and ran to the front door. That could only mean one thing. Martin was home.

She rushed to the kettle and put the water on. Then the door opened and Oolong let out a single happy bark in greeting. Sometimes they raced to greet Martin first, but Oolong's stubby little legs propelled him like a bullet. He was always the victor unless she distracted him with the hummingbird honey dispenser.

Angry squawks followed the next bark. She glanced out the window in time to see the flock of seagulls take to the air while Oolong chased the last gull across the sand. She hurried into the entryway where Martin finished hanging up his coat. He smiled when he spotted her, lifting the bag in his hand. "I got everything on your list." He set the bag down and pulled a stack of envelopes from his coat. Even on his honeymoon he was popular. "My father also a sent a letter. He congratulated me on my success." His chest puffed up. "He said my latest kettle has made the Steepe family a household name, and he is proud."

Charlotte smiled. "I'm glad he's finally recognized your hard work."

"Apparently Bertram is not taking well to his exile in the countryside, but it is better than him remaining in jail. Still a bit harsh I think, but when it's finally over, I'm sure we can all agree it was nothing but a tempest in a teapot," Charlotte couldn't agree, thinking how Bertram deserved to rot away in a cold dark cell. And yet for all the trouble he'd caused, he'd really only ended up hurting his own business interests. The stolen treasures were quietly returned, and Martin's father had managed to keep the scandal out of the public eye, so even the family's reputation hadn't suffered. Perhaps Martin was right after all.

"And that reminds me, the paperwork on Hawke has gone through. Mary is now the official owner."

Her heart leaped. Twilight at Hallow Manor continued to grow in popularity. Now Mary could grow Hawke too.

"Oh, but I did promise to not talk business while we're here. We'll save Hawke for when we return home." He gave her an apologetic smile and shoved the mail aside.

The kettle whistled. "Have a seat. I have a surprise for you for our afternoon tea." She dashed back off to the kitchen. It took her a moment to find the right tea. She'd made sure to slip it into his pile of tins for just such an occasion.

She met him out on the deck with the tea tray. The deck had become a favorite spot for both of them since arriving the day before. The early October weather made the air too cold for her to want to dip her toes into the sea, but walking up and down the beach proved peaceful.

"Are you enjoying the cottage?" he asked as she set the tray down on the little table between them.

"Yes. We should come back here in the spring when the weather warms."

"Would you like me to buy it? Then you can come as often as you please. You could use it as a writing retreat." He started to stand up, and she set a hand on his arm, unable to fight her amused smile. "No business talk, remember?"

"Right, sorry. Not another word until we're home," he promised. "Once Bertram returns, I will show you the family's country retreat." His smile fell, the side of his mouth twitching.

"No more Bertram talk either. It makes you sad. We are here to be happy." She scooped out a slice of the tart and set the plate in front of him. "An orange chocolate bakewell tart. The tea will be ready soon." She scooped her own serving.

Martin took a bite, making a small pleased moan as he ate. "I could eat your baking every day, but you don't need to work so hard when we are here to relax."

"I thought it would help me think. Mary loved my meat pie recipe, but agrees that I need to write something that won't be compared to The String of Pearls."

"Then why not write about something else you know? Like The Great Exhibition. Or tea." He scooped up a large bite of tart

"Hmm." The short mystery they'd followed had been exciting. "A mystery penny blood, then. I'll have to find a way to work my recipe in." That'd been her favorite part about her last story. She poured the tea, mulling over her experience chasing down Bertram's trail. A detective story. Or maybe a rivalry between businesses. No, no, an evil, scheming cousin. The tension would be great for a penny blood serial.

"This tart would pair perfectly with Charlotte's tea."

"That is precisely what I originally had in mind, but I made you something else instead."

Intrigued, Martin sniffed at his tea. "A black tea." He took a small sip, his eyebrows rising. "Is this Golden Monkey?"

"Yes. You once told me what it is good for, and I thought it would be perfect for this evening." After all, there was nowhere they needed to be tomorrow. No reason to rush out of bed in the morning like the day after their wedding to make it to the seaside.

"Oh Lottie," he purred. He caressed the side of her jaw with his thumb. "That is a hint I understand."

Epilogue

Dear Mary,
   Now that you know the story behind my inspiration for Charlotte's Tart, here is the recipe you wanted. Don't forget to drink it alongside Charlotte's Tea! Martin can't get enough of this pairing.

Frangipane:

- 1 cup orange marmalade
- 6 tablespoons unsalted butter
- 1/2 cup sugar
- 3/4 cup almond flour
- 2 tablespoons flour
- 1 large egg
- 1 large egg white
- 1 teaspoon vanilla extract
- 2 teaspoon almond extract
- Pinch of salt

Chocolate Ganache:

- 1/2 cup heavy whipping cream
- 1 bar semi-sweet baker's chocolate

Instructions:

Line a tart pan with pastry dough. Blind bake the crust at 350 degrees for 10 minutes. Use pie weights to keep the crust from bubbling.

To make the frangipane layer, beat together the butter, sugar, and salt until fluffy. Stir in the flours, whole egg, egg white, and extracts.

Once the crust has cooled, spread an even layer of your favorite orange marmalade across the tart. Spoon the almond mixture over the marmalade, spreading it to the edges of the tart. Bake for another 25 minutes.

Once the tart has baked, make the chocolate ganache by pouring simmering cream over the chocolate. You can break the chocolate into small pieces to help it melt. Top the tart with the ganache. For decoration you can top the tart with candied orange slices before serving.

The End

If you enjoyed this book please consider leaving a review. To stay up to date on my latest book news, join my newsletter (katevalentauthor.com/steeping-notes/)

About the Author

Kate Valent is three cats in a trench coat masquerading as a writer. She lives in Pennsylvania. She loves tea, history, and magic. You can learn more about Kate at katevalentauthor.com